I0557448

DEADLY HEARTBREAK

A
GEORGIA RAE WINSTON
MYSTERY

MARISSA SHROCK

CIMELIA PRESS

Deadly Heartbreak

© 2021 by Marissa Shrock

All rights reserved.

Cover art © Jennifer Zemanek/Seedlings Design Studio

Scriptures taken from the Holy Bible, New International Version®, NIV®. Copyright © 1973, 1978, 1984, 2011 by Biblica, Inc.™ Used by permission of Zondervan. All rights reserved worldwide. www.zondervan.com The "NIV" and "New International Version" are trademarks registered in the United States Patent and Trademark Office by Biblica, Inc.™

Published by Cimelia Press, Greentown, Indiana

Printed in the United States of America

Print ISBN-13: 978-0-9969879-7-4

Library of Congress Control Number: 2021903645

Be strong and take heart, all you who hope in the Lord.

Psalm 31:24

CHAPTER ONE

A long time ago, Daddy told me, "Georgia Rae, you'll rue the day you become addicted to caffeine."

Though I ignored his warning, I knew in my heart he was right, and the moment he'd predicted arrived one sticky August morning. I was sitting in my truck, parked down the street from Latte Conspiracies in my hometown of Wildcat Springs, Indiana. I was out of coffee and in dire need of an iced Area 51 Latte from my favorite joint. Because I'd waited for the Saturday morning rush to dissipate, the beginnings of a headache were knocking on my skull.

However, to obtain the life-sustaining beverage, I first needed to conquer my fear.

For normal, thirty-one-year-old adults, buying a cup of joe was no big deal, but in a small town, sometimes personal situations complicated what should've been insignificant matters. Several weeks ago, I'd broken up with the shop owner's son, Hamlet Miller. And last time there'd been issues between Hamlet and me, Bobbi Sue had practically jumped across the counter to confront me in front of the entire shop.

1

After this very dramatic incident, she'd apologized, but I still thought I had a legitimate reason for being apprehensive since I'd reunited with Detective Cal Perkins soon after ending my relationship with Hamlet.

Not many people knew Cal and I were back together—including some of my family—but I felt certain Bobbi Sue had gotten the scoop from someone. She had a knack for that.

Flicking my honey-blond braid back and forth between my fingers, I stared at the traffic passing through the one-stoplight town while I listened to the United Methodist Church bell tower chime "How Firm a Foundation."

I needed to get over myself. After all, the split had been mutual, and I was acting like Hamlet was pining away when he'd probably already forgotten me.

Thump, thump, thump.

My friend Ashley Choi stood waving next to my truck, and I opened the window.

"Good morning," I said. "What's going on?"

She leaned against the door and studied me, concern flooding her dark eyes. "I'm on my way to the studio, hon. Why're you just sitting here fiddling with your hair?"

"I'm trying to get up my nerve to go into Latte Conspiracies."

"Because you don't want to run into Hamlet?"

"Because I don't want Bobbi Sue to kill me."

"I see." She tossed her black hair over her shoulder and glanced at her phone. "I have time before my first class. How about I go in with you?"

I launched out of my truck before Ashley could change her mind.

"I'll take that as a *yes*."

"The coffee's on me," I said.

"I'm good, but thanks."

Such restraint.

Even with my protective detail, I entered the shop and approached the stainless-steel counter with a good dose of lingering trepidation. A few customers were scattered around the tables, and French doors led to Miller's Books—which Bobbi Sue's husband Hemingway ran.

Individual clipboards on the wall described each of the specialty drinks which included things like the Elvis Sighting Latte, the Crop Circle Cappuccino, and the Sasquatch Mocha. The exposed ductwork gave the shop an industrial vibe.

Bobbi Sue and Hemi's sixteen-year-old son Holden was restocking coffee cups with the shop's alien-print logo. He was short but sturdy and wore a gray and blue Wildcat Springs Tennis T-shirt with black athletic shorts.

He smiled and waved. "Hi, Georgia!"

"Hey!" He didn't look like he hated me. That was a good sign of my status with the Miller family.

A tanned, twenty-something guy I'd never seen working here greeted us. His wavy hair displayed perfect blond highlights, and it was clear from the way he sauntered to the counter that he thought he was hot stuff.

"What can we make for you lovely ladies?" Hot Stuff asked with a toothy grin.

"Iced Area 51 Latte—large." I glanced around. Where was Bobbi Sue? "Are you sure you don't want anything, Ashley?"

"On second thought, I'll have a Moon Landing Mocha," she said.

"Coming right up." Hot Stuff took my money and loyalty card.

"Where's your mom, Holden?" I needed to be prepared in case Bobbi Sue came flying out of the back room.

"She took the morning off." He began preparing our order.

I tried not to let my relief show and wished he'd given me

more details because it was pretty unusual for her not to be in the shop.

Was something wrong with Hamlet?

"How's Hamlet?" Ashley asked, as if she could read my mind.

Holden looked back and forth between us. "Fine."

A couple of awkward minutes passed before Hot Stuff held out a cup. "Moon Landing Mocha." He said the drink name as if he were a wannabe game-show announcer.

Ashley took her beverage. "I haven't seen you around here before. Are you new in town?"

"I am." He offered a dazzling smile. "Wolfe Sommers."

"Ashley Choi." She removed a business card from her yellow crossbody bag. "I run Joy of Imagination Art Studio. If you're ever interested in taking a class, it makes a fun date night for you and someone special."

"I'll keep that in mind." As Wolfe tucked the card in his apron pocket, his eyes fastened on her left hand—and the diamond engagement ring my cousin J.T. had given Ashley last weekend—before he raked his gaze over me.

"Maybe you and I could take a class together," he said.

Merciful heavens. Wolfe was clearly on the prowl. "That's nice of you, but—"

"She has a boyfriend—who's a cop." The normally sweet Ashley iced him with a fierce glare.

Holden looked over at us. Maybe the Millers *hadn't* heard about me getting back together with Cal.

"Too bad. We could've had a good time." Wolfe's gaze darkened as he surveyed me again before turning his focus to Ashley. "I'll have to check out one of your classes. I loved to draw when I was in school." He handed me my drink. "My art teacher always told me I had talent." He winked as if he wanted to let me know what I'd lost, and I fought my gag reflex.

We high-tailed it out of the shop and into the steamy heat.

"Where'd Bobbi Sue dig *him* up? I feel like I need a decontamination unit," I said as we stopped in front of the shop. "And by the way, if you weren't wearing that rock on your left hand, he'd have been after you."

"I noticed." She looked sheepish. "I promise I didn't mean to flirt. I'm just trying to drum up more customers."

"I know. How *has* business been?"

"Steady—with all the summer workshops for the kids. But I'd like to get more adults interested, so I'm going to have a booth at the Wildcat Arts Festival where I can display class information." She sipped her coffee. "Would you be willing to help out on Saturday? Pretty please? With sugar on top?"

"I'd be happy to."

"You're the best." She checked her phone. "I have to go because I have ten eight-year-olds coming for a painting workshop in a half hour."

"Ten eight-year-olds that I'm confident can out paint me."

Ashley laughed—but didn't argue. "Catch you later, hon." She strolled up the sidewalk toward her studio.

"Georgia!" A thin woman waving a napkin burst out of the coffee shop.

She wore a low-cut black and aqua tennis dress along with a generous amount of makeup. From the fine lines on her face, I guessed she was in her late forties but pegged her as the type who thought she could pass for late thirties.

"You and your friend slipped out when I wasn't looking, but I can't blame you with the way that *naughty* barista was flirting." She giggled and adjusted her white visor. "Oh, how I miss those days of being hit on."

I found it unbelievable that a woman wearing a short dress that displayed a generous portion of cleavage had left her days of being hit on behind.

But what'd I know?

"Now I have to take the initiative myself," she said.

That I could believe.

"Speak of the devil. It must be break time." Her gaze lingered on Wolfe, who was sauntering toward a white convertible.

I glanced around for an escape route, and she must've sensed I was about ready to bolt, because she tore her gaze from Wolfe and grasped my forearm.

"I'm glad I caught you."

Who *was* this woman? She looked vaguely familiar. "Ma'am?"

"Diana Graham." She lifted her chin, clearly communicating that my lack of recognition offended her. "From Liberty Christian Church."

Cal's church. I'd been with him once since we'd gotten back together, though I'd visited a handful of times when we'd dated before.

"I play the piano." Diana arched a sculpted eyebrow.

"Oh yes. And you do a fine job." She'd played a rousing version of "What a Friend We Have in Jesus" for the offertory last Sunday.

She released her grip on my arm. "Now that you're attending our church with your *gorgeous* hunk of a boyfriend, you're going to play the piano for me tomorrow."

I nearly choked on my latte—for so many reasons. "I—"

"It's short notice, but I have an important work deadline that has to be met by Monday morning. God will have to understand that I simply *must* break the Sabbath this week."

Yet she obviously had time to play tennis today. *Nice Georgia.* "I'm—"

"Normally, the pastor's wife subs for me, but she's at church camp with the kiddos this week, and if she can't, there are a couple of other people who can help, but they're on vacation. I heard through the grapevine you were trained as a music teacher and know how to play."

"That's true, and I'd be—"

"These are the hymn numbers." She thrust the napkin at me, and I had no choice but to take it. "Be there at 8:30 to run through them with the organist."

With her short skirt flipping, she flitted away, leaving a befuddled pianist in her wake.

———

That night, Cal dropped a batt of pink fiberglass insulation onto his attic floor, dimpled, and held both hands in surrender. "I swear I didn't say anything to Diana about you."

I set the insulation I was holding next to the other batts we'd carried up and put my hands on my hips. "Are you *sure*?" I followed him out of the stuffy attic, through his bedroom, and down to his newly remodeled kitchen where our pizza was almost finished baking.

"Absolutely. I learned a while ago, it's best to avoid Diana at all costs." He wrapped his arms around my waist. Cal's tall, muscular frame always made me feel petite, because I was too tall for my own good. With his dark hair and blue eyes, he was gorgeous. And had I mentioned the dimple?

"I appreciate your help with the insulation, by the way." He brushed a strand of hair from my face. "This old house needs it."

He wasn't going to get me off track. Though, I had a pretty good idea what he meant. "Why do you avoid Diana?"

"She threw herself at me the first Sunday I visited my church. Rumor has it she likes younger men, and I got the feeling that if I didn't steer clear, I'd find myself on a date with her without knowing how. That happened to another single guy."

"That's exactly how I felt. I'm the substitute pianist and don't know how it happened." I took two Coke cans from the refrigerator. "If you didn't tell Diana about me, then who did?"

"Pastor Jim? A lot of people in this community know you're talented after you directed the choir for your church Christmas program." His eyes gleamed. "It's fun watching you try to solve this mystery. It's the harmless kind that I can fully support you getting answers to." He kissed me, and between that and his sexy, resonant voice, I was about ready to melt.

I'd been involved in several murder investigations with the Richard County Sheriff's Department that were anything but harmless, and Cal and I had met when I'd found a body while harvesting soybeans last fall. Earlier this year, he'd even helped solve my daddy's murder—a case that'd been cold for nearly ten years.

"I suppose." I plopped onto a barstool. "Diana's putting a lot of faith in a total stranger. She didn't even check to see if I was free. She just assumed."

Cal's Miniature Schnauzer, Miss Peacock, wandered in and rested at my feet. He hadn't had the heart to rename the black dog he'd inherited from his great-aunt Beverly.

"You don't mind playing, do you?"

"Not at all." I'd planned to make Cal's church my own, so there was nothing like jumping in and getting involved.

He took the ham and pineapple pizza he'd made, entirely from scratch, out of the oven and set it on a hot pad. I was lucky that Cal liked to cook, because my specialty was microwave popcorn.

"I heard from Mason today," he said.

I sat up straighter. "Has there been a break in Natalie's case?"

Before Cal moved to Wildcat Springs, he'd worked as a detective in Cleveland with Mason Thrailkill. A few months ago, Mason's wife Natalie had been murdered while riding her bike on a trail near their home.

"Unfortunately, no," he said. "But Mason's been in Cleveland getting his house cleaned out and put on the market, and he wants to swing through Indiana to see us on his way back to Atlanta. He'll be here Thursday."

"Cool. I've been wanting to meet him. Is he moving to Atlanta?"

"Yes. His grandma has been a big help with babysitting Henry, and Mason decided they could use a fresh start." He ran a cutter through the pizza. "It'll be good to see him again."

"I can't wait to hear some stories about you."

Cal chuckled. "He could tell you plenty." He handed me a plate. "Help yourself, my brown-eyed girl."

"You don't have to tell me twice." Homemade pizza, a movie, and my handsome boyfriend.

Life was absolutely perfect.

CHAPTER TWO

W hile I drove my truck to Liberty Christian Church, I took in the flat, fertile land covered by corn and soybean fields with the occasional house or barn dotting the landscape. The humid morning promised another scorching day, and I said yet another silent prayer for rain because my crops could use a good soaking.

A gray sedan approached from the opposite direction, taking more than its share of the narrow county road. I slowed and drove onto the berm to avoid sideswiping the car. "Seriously? I'm bigger than you." I tried to get a look at the driver, but the sun's glare blocked my view. I scowled and bit back the name I really wanted to call the maniac.

But I wasn't going to let road rage ruin this beautiful Sunday.

Squeezing the steering wheel, I continued on until I arrived at the charming, old-fashioned church with a steeple. Mature maple trees surrounded the building, and to the north was a small cemetery.

I parked and hurried inside, where light streamed through stained-glass onto dark wooden pews. The organist was nowhere to be found, so I stood for a second at the back of the sanctuary. This would be a beautiful place for a wedding. The church I'd been attending, Wildcat Springs Community Church, was Bible-based and vibrant, but I had no desire to get married in an auditorium.

But I was getting ahead of myself. Still, I was determined that, this time around, Cal and I would get our relationship right.

While I waited on the organist, I went to the piano and played the hymns Diana had given me. The hymnal was the same one I had at home, and I was used to each version. When I finished and looked up, Cal was sitting in the first pew, and he applauded.

"Pastor Jim told me the organist is sick, so you're on your own."

"No problem." I'd pick a few of my favorite hymns for the offering time.

He stood and laced his fingers through mine. "I love that dress. You look gorgeous."

"Thanks." I was wearing a new black and white sundress.

We headed downstairs to the adult Sunday school room where folks of all ages sat at long tables arranged in a U shape. We greeted everyone, found two empty folding chairs, and Cal went to the kitchen to get coffee for us. A tall, mousy looking woman slipped into the seat next to the one I'd saved for Cal.

"Good morning," I said. "I'm—"

"Cal's girlfriend." If the basement classroom hadn't already had a hint of a chill, her monotone and unsmiling face would've cooled it instantly.

"That's right."

"You're playing the piano for the service."

"Right again." I removed a sweater from my handbag and tugged it on.

She pushed up her tortoise shell glasses. "Diana should've asked me. I know how to play."

Life Lesson #899: In nearly every small church, there's a battle for the piano bench.

I hadn't signed up for *that*. "Listen, I'm sorry. Diana tracked me down yesterday on the street and asked, and I didn't have an opportunity to say no. I didn't mean to overstep. I was helping because I thought it's what the church needed, so if you—"

"There's no need to babble." She ran her thumb back and forth over the gilded Bible pages. "You've practiced. You should play."

Her stony words made me glad I'd slipped on my sweater.

"Hey there, Arden," Cal said.

Arden's face broke into a huge smile, and she removed her glasses. "Good morning, Cal. I've been getting to know your sweet girlfriend. How's work?"

While my head spun from her rapid change in demeanor, he set a Styrofoam cup in front of each of us, and a glazed donut between us. "Busy as usual."

I recognized Cal's cordial-but-not-too-friendly tone.

He sat beside her, and she rested her hand on his arm. I had to fight the urge to reach over and shove it away.

Nice Georgia.

"I've been writing a mystery novel, and I've read about a lot of your cases." Arden batted her eyes. "I was wondering if I could observe you like on *Castle*. I want my detective to be strong and intelligent, and you're very good at what you do."

No wonder she'd taken off her glasses. If she hadn't, her lashes would've streaked the lenses like bad windshield wipers. Me-*ow*.

Nice Georgia was AWOL.

Lord, forgive me. I stuffed a bite of donut in my mouth. Cal had better hurry if he wanted a piece.

"If you're looking for a Kate Beckett type, then you'll want to model your character after my partner, Vanessa Hawk-Remington," he said. "I'll give her your name, and she can touch base with you and answer your questions."

Well played, Calvin. Well. Played.

"I'd appreciate that." Her friendly tone had grown frosty. She flashed what I sensed was a fake smile, then put on her glasses and opened her Bible.

———

My stint as the temporary pianist was a success, though Arden had sat behind Cal and shot hate beams in my direction for the entire service. After church, Cal and I beat the lunch crowd to Velda's Café in downtown Wildcat Springs. The shop had a vintage chic look with mismatched chairs and tables. Historical photos taken around our town hung on the buttery yellow walls.

We ordered sandwiches, and I snagged a table in the corner near the window while Cal waited for our food at the counter.

"So, what's the story with Arden?" I asked as Cal set my turkey wrap on the table along with his roast beef sandwich.

"She's a sweet person who hasn't lived here that long. I tried to be welcoming when she started attending our church, because I know what it's like to be the new guy." He scooted out a chair and sat.

Sweet person? Were we talking about the same woman? "And?"

"You assume there's more?"

"My female intuition insists there's more." Well, that and Arden's clear disdain for me—when Cal wasn't looking—made it incredibly obvious.

"Are you jealous?"

"Not at all."

He put his napkin on his lap. "Ever since we met, Arden has gone out of her way to talk to me at church, and one week she even brought me homemade cinnamon rolls."

"Were they good?"

"I've had better."

Smart answer.

"When she asked me out a few weeks ago, I said yes. I wasn't interested but thought if we had a date, she'd see we didn't click. But you and I got back together a few days later, so I cancelled our date—and apologized."

"How'd she take it?"

"Fine, I think."

"You *think?*"

"She must not be that upset if she wanted to observe me."

Men. "She's not acting upset because she thinks she still has a chance."

"Really?"

Merciful heavens. "Uh-huh. If you didn't pick up on that, then why'd you recommend that she observe Vanessa instead?"

"Because it'd be awkward having her watch me knowing that I might've hurt her feelings when I turned her down. Was I tactful enough?" Concern lingered in his eyes.

"Absolutely." I reached for his hand, and he quickly blessed our food. I lifted my head. "While you were getting our coffee, Arden lamented that nobody had asked her to play the piano. Obviously, I had no idea. I was just doing what Diana Graham told me to do."

"It's not your fault."

"Next time I see Diana, I'll tell her about Arden," I said. "She should have a turn playing if she's any good." I hoped this would smooth things over with Arden.

"Incoming," Cal whispered as I took a bite.

"I see the rumors are true. You hardly let the dust settle after your breakup with Hammie before you got back together with *him*." Bobbi Sue Miller stopped next to our table, and her wiry and mustachioed husband Hemi hovered behind her. Instead of her usual novelty T-shirt and jeans, she wore navy capri pants with a flowy, white blouse, and a flying saucer pendant necklace, so I figured they'd been to church.

"Afternoon, ma'am, sir," Cal said.

"Well, Georgia?" Bobbi Sue put her hands on her hips. "What do you have to say for yourself?"

I swallowed and chose my words carefully, because the people of Wildcat Springs didn't need another episode of the *Bobbi Sue and Georgia Rae Show*. "Hamlet's a wonderful man, but we wanted different things, so it was best to go our separate ways."

"Hmph. Seems disrespectful to me." She crossed her arms. "Flaunting your new relationship all over town."

Cal and I had hardly flaunted our relationship, but she was certainly entitled to her view. "I'm sorry. Is Hamlet okay?"

She narrowed her eyes. "Do you think he's sitting around moping? There are other fish in the sea."

"Bobbi Sue." Hemi rested a hand on his wife's shoulder.

"I didn't mean it that way." I cast a pleading glance at Cal.

"Ma'am, my girlfriend and I would like to eat in peace," Cal said. "So, if you don't have anything pleasant to say, I'd appreciate it if you and your husband would go enjoy your lunch."

My hero.

"We'll get out of your hair." Hemi's understanding smile reminded me of Hamlet.

Bobbi Sue huffed. "I'm sorry, Georgia. Hamlet *did* make us think he was going to be content flipping houses. I should've known my boy wouldn't be happy not acting. The bug bit him in junior high, and he hasn't been the same since. Heaven knows, you belong here on your farm."

"I love it."

"I guess having you as my daughter-in-law was always wishful thinking," she said. "*I'd* have been a good mother-in-law." She glanced at Cal, then back at me. "I met his mother when she was in town visiting, and let's just say, I wish you luck."

Inwardly, I cringed. Cal coughed but otherwise appeared undaunted. To say Yvonne, a retired police detective, was a piece of work would be an understatement of epic proportions, though I was certain her tenacity had played a small role in getting Cal to rethink his decision to shut me out of his life.

"Enjoy your lunch." Bobbi Sue grasped her husband's hand and sailed into line.

Amusement danced in Cal's eyes.

So he had an overbearing mother. Not everything about him could be perfect, could it?

When Cal and I finished eating, I hopped into my oven of a truck, peeled off my sweater, and buzzed out of town with my windows sealed tight and the air conditioning vents pointed at my face. A recording of my stepsister's college choir performing "The Water is Wide" played on my sound system.

The road that led to my century-old farmhouse was lined with tall stalks of corn, tassels and leaves swaying in the breeze. I adored Indiana in the summer, even with the oppressive humidity.

When I got home, I hurried into the house, released my yellow Labrador retriever Gus from his crate, and fastened his leash. I didn't have time for monkey business this afternoon because I was hosting my Bible study group this evening, and my house needed a good cleaning.

I opened my back door, but it thumped against something

solid that hadn't been on the porch when I'd let Gus out this morning.

I pushed harder, and the barrier slid away. Peeking outside, I spotted a cardboard box with large pink heart stickers plastered all over. On one side, someone had printed *GEORGIA RAE* in sloppy handwriting.

Had Cal left me a present? No, this wasn't his style, and he typically didn't use my middle name. Most people didn't unless they were mad at me. Had Ashley sent a gift? She often called me by both names.

Gus wiggled past me and sniffed the box.

"What do you think, buddy?"

He looked at me, then resumed snooping.

The tape job looked thorough, so I'd need a knife. I stooped and picked up the box, which was fairly light considering the size, and a wet patch remained where the package had been.

Weird.

As I straightened, the bottom gave way, and a massive hunk of raw meat plopped onto the porch.

CHAPTER THREE

"Ugh!" I jumped and tossed the box aside. Gus lunged for the rotund chunk and licked it. "No!" I yanked his leash, but he strained in the opposite direction and clamped his teeth into the bloody lump.

Ripping the slimy meat from his mouth, I threw it aside, wrestled my dog into the kitchen, and slammed the door behind us. With his tail wagging, he chomped a morsel as if he were challenging me to take it. "Gus!" I wailed. "We don't know what's in that! Merciful heavens, you crazy animal!"

In spite of the fact that I was still wearing my new dress, I dove for my dog, caught him, and pried open his mouth. As he wriggled and made gagging noises, I dug out the piece and tossed it into my sink with a splat.

I darted onto the porch and closed the door. Gus's head popped up, and he woofed at me through the window. Bending down, I examined the red mass that was roughly the size of my head and covered with creamy fat patches.

I was pretty certain it was a beef heart.

At least once a year, Grandpa paid one of his friends who

raised cattle to butcher a cow, and our family shared the many packages of beef. One year, I'd ended up with the heart, and I had no idea how that'd happened, because my experience with beef was limited to cooking taco meat, frying hamburger patties, and grilling steak.

Could Arden be that upset over losing her chance with Cal? Surely, she wouldn't do something this gross if she wanted to stay on his good side.

Unless she was crazy.

She would've had time to package and deliver the heart while Cal and I were eating, and she'd left quickly after the worship service. But with all the moisture that'd seeped through the box, the heart must've spent time in someone's freezer, and the meat looked defrosted. If she'd taken it out of her freezer after church, would it have thawed that quickly? Probably not, unless she'd planned ahead, which was possible because she knew about me before our official meeting in Sunday school.

I chewed my lip and considered other suspects. Had my twin stepbrothers Preston and Austin found the heart in our parents' freezer and decided to mess with me? But that seemed like a stretch for two twenty-five-year-old pretty-boy real estate agents, who probably never thought about where their meat came from. Even if they *were* ornery.

Gus barked again. He seemed fine, but if my stepbrothers weren't responsible, then I should call the vet. I tapped out a group text to the twins.

Did you guys leave a present on my back porch today?

Preston's answer slid onto my phone.

We're not that nice. Maybe u have a secret admirer.

Austin's response appeared.

If it's your birthday, the answer is YES!!!!

I gave the heart a little shove with my foot, nudging it closer to the box before I snapped a picture and sent it to them.

If you're messing with me, this isn't funny. It's gross.

Preston answered within seconds.

What even is that????!!!!

My fingers flew across the screen.

A beef heart.

I snorted at Preston's reply.

Like from a cow?

Where did he think beef came from? I included a cow emoji with my answer.

Yes. Moo.

Austin answered with a barfing emoji.

We'll be there in fifteen.

I knew better than to protest because that'd make them more determined to show up. Stepping off my porch, I shaded my eyes and strolled around the house to my front yard. Down the road,

Cal was mowing his lawn, and he didn't always carry his phone when he was working outside.

Since the Twin Menaces were on the way, I called Cal, and when he didn't answer, I left a message for him to get back with me but didn't mention the heart. I could go get him, but he could deal with this later, and a gross prank didn't need to interrupt his peaceful Sunday afternoon.

Did it?

While I waited for my stepbrothers to arrive, I let Gus out and changed into denim capris and a tank top before stowing the heart on a disposable plate beside the box on my kitchen table. Then, I scrubbed my hands and called the emergency number for Dr. Tiffany Brown at Heartland Animal Hospital—as a precaution. Gus was scampering through my house like a crazy dog, but I wanted to know what signs to look for in case some sicko had poisoned the heart.

"I've heard about some of your close calls," she said after I'd explained the situation. "Are you in the middle of an investigation?"

"No. Which is why this whole thing is weird."

"Huh. If Gus vomits, has diarrhea, won't eat, or acts lethargic, call me right away."

Gus blew by me while he ran thundering laps between my kitchen and living room. "He's definitely not lethargic."

"It sounds like your buddy's just fine. Good luck solving this mystery, and call if you have any more questions."

Dr. Brown disconnected, and I looked at Gus, who'd stopped running.

"I don't know, Gus. What do you think?"

He panted, walked to his water dish, and slurped.

So helpful.

Preston and Austin burst through my back door into the kitchen. They were blond, broad-shouldered former football players who never lacked for female attention. Today, they were wearing shirts and ties, so they must've had open houses this afternoon. Austin had recently grown a goatee, and I guessed it was because they were getting tired of people mixing them up—though I knew the secret.

Austin had a scar by his eye from where he'd fallen as a kid.

"Are you okay?" they asked in unison. Then, they turned toward each other and grinned. "Jinx!"

"Weirded out but fine," I said.

Preston examined the heart. "Do people actually eat these?" He looked like he was about two seconds from barfing up his lunch.

"Yep. Mom once told me it's a good source of iron. I could call her and ask the best way to fix it." I pointed to the divot. "Gus enjoyed his piece."

"Hard pass." Austin looked pale. "It comes from a cow, right?"

"Pretty sure. Look at it. It's way too big to be a human heart."

"Uh . . . right. I knew that." Austin glanced at his brother. "We'll be your sidekicks and help you find the Cow-Heart Creeper."

Preston gave him a high-five. "Dude, that's an awesome name."

I laughed. "That *is* a good name."

Austin grinned. "See, you *do* love us."

"Don't get carried away," I said.

Preston pointed at the box. "What's that paper sticking out from underneath the box?"

"I didn't see it before." I grabbed a napkin and carefully slid the damp paper out. The ink had bled, but the sloppily printed message was legible. "A dead heart for Georgia Rae, the Heart-breaker." I dropped the note onto the table. "Wow."

"Maybe Cal's upset about your relationship with Hamlet," Preston said.

"Dude, he wouldn't do something like this." Austin elbowed his brother.

"So . . . update," I said. "Hamlet decided to go back to acting. Since he's going to be moving around, and I don't want to leave Wildcat Springs, we broke up. Cal and I are actually dating again."

"Wait, what?" they said in unison.

"We've got to stop that," Austin muttered.

"When did this development happen, and why didn't you tell us?" Preston folded his arms.

"A couple of weeks ago. And do you send me play-by-plays of *your* love lives?"

"But this is a highlight," Preston said. "I'm wounded." He pretended to stab himself and staggered backward with a dramatic groan.

"Same here." Austin moaned and clutched his chest.

I rolled my eyes.

Austin inspected the box without touching it. "Hamlet wouldn't have done this, would he?"

"No way. The breakup was mutual." Uncertainty rippled through my gut. Bobbi Sue *claimed* Hamlet was fine, but what if he wasn't, and that's why she'd accosted me earlier?

Preston surveyed me. "Didn't he always call you Georgia Rae?"

"Yes. But he's too much of a gentleman to do something this twisted."

"What about his mom? Isn't she weird?" Austin asked.

"She's quirky and isn't afraid to confront you when she has a" —I snickered and pointed at the heart— "*beef* with you."

The twins guffawed, and when they settled down, I told them about what'd happened at Velda's Café. "My gut feeling is Bobbi Sue said her peace and has accepted Hamlet's choice." Of course, she hadn't resisted getting in a dig about Cal's mom, so I might've been giving her too much credit. She could've delivered the heart *before* accosting me at Velda's.

"Have you broken any other hearts we don't know about?" Austin asked.

I considered my encounter at the coffee shop. "Yesterday, the new barista at Latte Conspiracies asked me out. He may've been offended when I said no, but it'd be arrogant to assume I broke his heart."

"What's his name?" Preston looked ready to hunt him down.

"Wolfe Sommers. He's new in town, so how would he know where I live? Let alone my middle name."

"There's no such thing as privacy anymore," Preston said. "He could find out a ton online. Or he's the psycho stalker type who can't take rejection from a woman."

Austin chuckled. "He's at the top of my list with a name like Wolfe."

"You guys are creeping me out."

Preston reexamined the box. "The package has pink heart stickers. What if we're coming at this the wrong way, and some girl's heartbroken that she lost her chance with Cal because of Georgia?"

"You could be on to something." I told them about Arden's behavior that morning and how my first thought was that she'd left the heart. "But I doubt she'd do something like this if she's hoping to change Cal's mind."

"Didn't Cal date that hot baker chick while you guys were broken up?" Austin asked. "What's her name?"

"Taryn Anderson. She owns Pastry Delight."

"Right," Preston said. "She might've heard you and Cal got back together, so she sent you a present because she's bitter."

I had to give them credit for thinking of someone I hadn't considered, and I certainly wasn't one of Taryn's favorite people. "You may be on to something. And . . ." I snapped my fingers. "Taryn's brother works in a meat processing facility. She could've gotten a heart from him."

Preston pointed toward the box. "With those girly stickers, my money's on Taryn the baker."

"She *does* like the color pink," I said. "It's all over her shop."

"But if she's a girly-girl, would she do something this gross?" Austin wrinkled his nose.

"Good point," I said. "I also don't see her lacking in the date department, and she's probably moved on from Cal."

Preston waggled his eyebrows. "Want me to find out?"

"Maybe *I* want to find out." Austin glared at him.

"One of you could ask Taryn, and the other could ask Arden." I smirked.

"I don't think so." Austin huffed.

"Forget it," Preston said. "We don't need crazy stalker chicks in our lives."

"That's what I thought. And speaking of crazy . . ." I told them about Diana Graham. "What if she wanted me to play the piano, so she'd know I was at church and it was safe to deliver the heart? She made the comment that Cal is gorgeous, and he told me she threw herself at him when he first started attending their church."

"We have a lot of suspects, sissy," Austin said.

I'd yet to break him of the habit of calling me that. "No kidding. Anyone I've ever made mad could've done this."

"What does Cal think?" Preston asked.

"He doesn't know yet because he's been mowing his yard. I left him a message."

Preston glanced at his brother. "You should go get him."

"Nah. This is a stupid prank. It's not like he's going to launch a criminal investigation. He'll get here when he gets here." I put my hands on my hips. "Are you aware that you're sounding more and more like your dad?"

My stepdad Dan was notoriously cautious and overprotective —though he was a nice man who made my mom happy.

Austin roared with laughter. "I said the same thing last week when he was fretting about Makayla's new boyfriend."

Preston bristled. "Since when is being protective a bad thing?"

"It's not," I said. "I have to give you guys a hard time, since you enjoy doing the same to me."

"Fair enough," Preston said. "And I'm going to continue channeling Dad and strongly suggest you get a video doorbell to enhance your security."

"Good idea." Mom and Dan had already purchased a home security system for me after someone had tried to kill me last fall.

"Do you want us to look around and make sure the boogeyman isn't hiding? We've got time before our open houses," Austin said.

"I'd appreciate that." Cal would insist on checking again when he arrived, but I didn't want to hurt my stepbrothers' feelings.

"I'll take the barns. Presty, take the house." Austin darted out the door to the garage.

As I put plastic wrap over the heart and deposited it in my refrigerator, Preston looked around my kitchen.

"Are you ever going to update?" he asked.

I took in the flower basket print wallpaper, laminate counter-top, and linoleum floor. "You mean you don't like my 1980s throwback?"

"You can do better."

"Updates cost money."

"Is that the issue? Or is it because you don't want to change your dad's renovation?" He opened my basement door, flipped on the light, and we filed into the musty depths.

"Who are you, and what've you done with Preston? I'm very weirded out right now."

"So I'm right." He opened the door to my tornado shelter and peeked in.

I liked it better when he was teasing me instead of psychoanalyzing me. "That might have something to do with it." I purchased this farmhouse from my mom when she married Dan, and I hadn't changed much except some furniture—and the chalk wall I painted in the dining room.

He peeked behind some boxes. "Your dad would want you to bring your kitchen into the twenty-first century." He tromped back up the stairs.

I followed. "How can you say that when you didn't even know him?"

"No father would want his daughter to stare at that atrocious wallpaper for years after it went out of style. At least rip it down and paint. That's not expensive."

"Fine. Maybe it *is* time for a change." I flicked off the light and closed the door. "When did you start shrinking heads?"

He barged through my foyer and upstairs to the second floor as I trailed behind.

"When I figured out it's another amazing way to keep you off balance." He stopped on the landing and winked.

That was more like it.

After Austin and Preston deemed my home safe and headed off to their open houses, I embarked on a cleaning frenzy while Gus snoozed in his doggie bed. It was almost five-thirty when Cal returned my call, and my friends were scheduled to arrive at six.

"Did you forget to buy ice?" he asked as soon as I answered.

"No. I got some yesterday. If you're ready, could you come early? There's something I want to talk to you about."

"I'll be right over."

He disconnected, and I peeked in the oven and checked the chicken spaghetti casseroles Cal had made the day before. The wonderful aroma filled my kitchen, and I was thrilled he'd offered to cook the main course, because I was tired of serving pizzas from the local joint. I had a feeling my friends were too.

For dessert, the pies I'd purchased at an Amish bakery when I was on vacation were thawed and ready to go.

Cal knocked on the back door, and I let him in.

"I promise to behave myself in front of your friends." He kissed me.

"I'm not worried about that. I . . . um . . . someone left a present for me today." While I gathered paper plates, napkins, and cups from my pantry, I told him about the heart and note.

He ran his fingers through his hair "Why didn't you come get me?"

"I thought about it, but I wondered if Preston and Austin were pranking me. When I asked them, they insisted on coming over, and Preston found the note. I wasn't in imminent danger and figured I'd tell you this evening."

"You didn't throw away the note or the box, did you?"

"You've trained me better than that. They're in the garage. No one has touched them but me, and the heart's in the refrigerator."

"Besides Bobbi Sue, have you made anyone mad lately?" He opened the fridge and peered inside. "There's a hunk missing. And teeth marks." He closed the door.

I pointed at Gus, and he thumped his tail against the floor. No remorse. Typical.

Cal's dimple appeared, and it took me a second to focus on answering his question. "The boys and I came up with several possibilities." I told him about Wolfe, Arden, Taryn, and Diana.

"Arden wouldn't do something like this."

I flinched. "Why not?"

"Because she's a sweet person."

I put my hands on my hips. "She wasn't acting sweet this morning until you showed up."

"Didn't you say she was hurt because Diana didn't ask her to play the piano?"

"Yes." Why was he certain Arden was innocent?

"Then that's probably all it was. Did Wolfe seem upset when you turned him down?"

"How do you know I turned him down?"

"Very funny. But seriously, how did he react?"

"He seemed offended that I wasn't interested." I opened the door to the garage and pointed at the workbench. "The box and note are over there."

Gus followed as Cal approached the workbench and examined the box without touching. "Interesting the person used your middle name. How many people call you Georgia Rae?"

"Hamlet. Ashley. My mom and Grandpa when they're mad." I swallowed. "Daddy *always* called me Georgia Rae."

"Do you think Hamlet could've done this?" he asked.

"Absolutely not, especially since we split on good terms."

"He's such a stand-up guy that it seems like a stretch to me too." Cal looked thoughtful. "Stop by the department tomorrow, so we can get elimination prints from you. I'll check the box, but we'll probably only find yours. Whoever did this likely wore gloves."

"You really think that's necessary?" I flicked off the garage light, and we returned to my kitchen.

"I do." His expression left no room for disagreement.

I wasn't going to argue, but I *was* going to keep telling myself this situation was no big deal. "Cal?"

"Yes?"

"Let's not mention this to my small group," I said. "I don't want anyone to worry."

"Everyone," my friend Brandi Hartfield said as she entered my kitchen through back door. "I'd like you to meet my new neighbor Arden Tanner. She recently moved here from Michigan."

Sweet baby Moses in a basket.

"Welcome!" I curled my fingers around an oven mitt and gave myself an A+ for how perky I sounded.

Cal, Ashley, and J.T. echoed my greeting while I mentally vowed to give Arden a chance. But my good intentions hit the road when I noticed she was wearing a Texas Rangers baseball cap. I was willing to bet that had everything to do with getting Cal's attention—since he'd been a pitcher for the team a couple of years after college.

Arden swept her gaze over everybody. "I already know Georgia—and Cal."

"Really?" Brandi glanced at me.

"I met Georgia during Sunday school this morning," Arden said. "She played the piano *beautifully* for our worship service."

Her syrupy words didn't match her unfriendly expression.

"I see." Brandi's mellow voice remained pleasant, though I knew her well enough to spot the uncertainty flickering in her green eyes when she glanced at me. "This is our newly engaged couple." She introduced J.T. and Ashley and looked at me. "I heard David, Heather, and Evan are out for tonight, but is Hamlet coming?"

"Here." The lanky but handsome Hamlet strolled through my back door—followed by Wolfe Sommers.

What in the world was happening right now? I hadn't even been certain Hamlet was going come, and he had to drag along Wolfe—of all people?

My evening kept getting better and better.

Hamlet gazed toward Arden with an expression on his chiseled face that I couldn't quite read. She studied her feet and fidgeted with her T-shirt's hem.

He motioned toward Wolfe. "This is Wolfe Sommers, who's not only playing Tommy Djilas in *The Music Man* but is also the newest employee at Latte Conspiracies." Hamlet had recently been cast as Harold Hill in the production at Bell's Dinner Theater in Richardville, so that explained their connection.

Wolfe's toothy grin spread over his face as he looked at me. "Remember me?"

"How could I forget?" Knowing Wolfe was an actor explained a lot.

Wolfe laughed with a little too much gusto, and I half expected him to flex his biceps for us.

Hamlet glanced at me. "It sounds like there's an interesting story here."

"Not really." I busied myself by taking casseroles out of the oven, but I felt my friends' eyes on me. I didn't mind inviting new people into the group—but a head's up would've been nice. We'd have plenty of food since Cal had doubled the chicken spaghetti recipe, but I could've used the chance to prepare mentally for this onslaught of weirdos, one of whom might or might not've deposited a beef heart on my back porch.

Nice Georgia. Jesus loves them, and so should you.

"I asked Georgia on a date yesterday, but apparently the pretty lady's already got a boyfriend." Wolfe winked.

Someone send a barf bag via express mail.

"I was there," Ashley said quickly. "That's *literally* all that happened."

Wolfe surveyed the men in the room. "Which one of you guys am I going to have to take out?"

"That'd be me." With an inscrutable expression on his face, Cal held out his hand. "*Detective* Cal Perkins."

Wolfe took Cal's offered hand but flinched.

The edge of my mouth twitched.

"Georgia isn't the only single girl in the world, and she's pretty, but it's not as if she's a supermodel." Arden snapped as she lifted her chin.

Yikes.

Cal did a double take. Maybe *now* he'd believe what I'd told him about Arden. Uncomfortable silence fell over my kitchen as Ashley and J.T. looked at their phones, and Hamlet studied his sandals. Brandi stared at her new neighbor as if she were having trouble comprehending how someone could be so rude to her hostess.

Wolfe laughed—again—and sidled up to Arden. "You and I should get to know each other. What's your name, spunky lady?"

"Call me Arden. I abhor nicknames." She stepped closer and gave him a taste of his own medicine by giving him an obvious once over. "You aren't my type. Spray tans are an abomination."

"I can be very persuasive." He held out his arm and examined it. "Besides, this is all the sun—and me."

"I'm not easily persuaded." Arden stared at him.

Why had I ever thought I'd cornered the market on awkwardness? I'd certainly had my uncomfortable moments through the years, but I wasn't even playing in the same league as these two. I frantically rooted through my utensil drawer for a serving spoon. When I found it hiding in the bottom, I waved it in victory.

"Supper's ready!" My voice was pitched a little too high to be normal. I shoved the spoon into one of the casseroles.

Wolfe peered at the chicken spaghetti and then looked at me. "If that tastes as good as it looks, I'm going to need that recipe. I love me some pasta."

"I—"

"I'd be happy to give it to you." Cal clasped his hand over Wolfe's shoulder. "Now, let's pray so we can dig in."

Good call. I needed all the prayer I could get.

A couple hours later, my friends and I had put a good dent in the casseroles and pies. J.T. had taught our Bible lesson, and Arden, Wolfe, and Hamlet didn't stick around when the lesson was finished. As soon as Arden and Wolfe left, I felt like I could breathe normally.

Cal invited J.T. to his house to hang out and watch major league baseball so Brandi, Ashley, and I could have some much-needed girl talk. We also wanted to discuss Ashley and J.T.'s wedding plans, since they'd set a date in June.

While Gus sniffed the kitchen floor for crumbs, I divided the remaining pie slices among four plates. My curvy figure did *not* need extra pie sitting around.

"I'm sorry about Arden." Brandi ripped a sheet of aluminum foil from the container and tucked it around her slices of apple and cherry pie. "I met her a couple of days ago after I came home from Europe and got the impression that she could use some friends. When I saw her this afternoon, I felt like God was prompting me to invite her. I had no idea she was so . . . candid."

"*Candid?* That's one way of putting it, hon." Ashley covered her pie. "Poor Georgia practically has bruises from that verbal bludgeoning."

"True story." I slid the last piece of cherry pie onto J.T.'s plate.

"But." Ashley held up a finger. "I predict she and Wolfe get together."

"Seriously? She said he isn't her type." I went to the sink, rinsed the pie server, and stuck it into the dishwasher.

"That's what she *said*. But she was totally checking him out during the lesson. She's playing hard to get because she's annoyed that Wolfe is such an obnoxious pretty boy."

"That's a good thing." As I wiped off the island, I told them about what'd happened at church that morning and how Cal had been blind to her true feelings about me.

"Ash, I hope you're right and she turns her attention to Wolfe," Brandi said. "She could be trouble, and Cal and Georgia don't need anyone messing up their relationship now that they're finally back together."

"Amen." I tried not to dwell on the beef heart sitting in my refrigerator. *Just a prank. Just a prank.*

"It's a good sign that Cal came to Bible study tonight." Brandi brushed her short brown curls out of her face. "Since he wasn't willing when you were dating before."

"We worked out a compromise," I said. "I'll attend his church, and he'll come to my Bible study group. He regretted not getting to know my friends better, and he wants to make an effort this time."

Brandi smiled. "I'm thrilled for you."

"Same," Ashley said. "You're glowing."

"I've never been this happy." As I said the words, a flutter of uncertainty rippled through my stomach, but I charged ahead. "Cal is everything I've been hoping and praying for, and this time, nothing's getting in the way of our relationship."

CHAPTER FOUR

Monday morning, I went to the sheriff's department in Richardville to get fingerprinted. Then, before the temperatures soared, I scouted fields with the drone I'd purchased a while back.

At first, Grandpa had thought the drone was ridiculous, especially when I'd had to get certified by the Federal Aviation Administration in order to operate it, but I liked adding the latest technology to my farming arsenal. The drone helped me check quickly for trouble spots in our corn and soybean fields. When I'd told Grandpa the drone would save us time and money in the long run, he was all in.

As I drove through Wildcat Springs on the way to the land Grandpa and I were cash renting from the Dillman family, I decided to make a quick stop. Even though I'd mostly convinced myself the beef heart wasn't a serious threat, the mystery-loving part of me still wanted to identify the Cow-Heart Creeper. So, I found a parking space on Main Street and strolled around the corner to Pastry Delight for my second breakfast.

Not only had Taryn Anderson dated Cal, but she'd also made

me mad enough that I'd boycotted her bakery, so I hadn't set foot in the place for months. But my desire for a chocolate chip cookie —or two—coupled with the need for information, caused me to change my mind.

I entered the shop—that looked like a pink unicorn had projectile vomited—and approached the bakery case while the door alert's tinny version of "Für Elise" announced my presence. But instead of Taryn and her perky blond topknot bouncing out of the back room, Arden plodded toward me, her face expressionless.

Life Lesson #12,999. The road to destruction is paved with chocolate chip cookies.

"What can I get you?" Arden's monotone had made a comeback.

I eyed the bakery case full of cakes, tarts, cookies, and other assorted pastries. "Two chocolate chip cookies."

She withdrew a paper wrapper from a cardboard box. "Do you want anything to drink?"

"A bottle of water, please."

She slipped the cookies in a pink bag and retrieved the water from a minifridge behind the counter. "I baked these cookies this morning." She handed them to me without a hint of pleasantness, in spite of being a guest in my home the night before.

"Is Taryn not here?" Perfect segue.

"She and her whole family are on a trip to the Grand Canyon."

"That's fun. Did her brother and his wife go too?" I hoped I sounded casual instead of like I was on a full-fledged fishing expedition.

"That's what I meant when I said, 'whole family.'" She took the bills I held out. "They left Thursday and will be back Wednesday. Taryn was excited. She's never been west of the Mississippi River." Arden dealt statements like playing cards.

"Good for her." Taryn most likely wasn't the Cow-Heart Creeper, unless she'd put Arden up to delivering the organ, which was entirely possible. "By the way, it's cool that you're working on a mystery novel. What's it about?"

"A former police detective moves from a big city to a small town and finds a dead body in the house she's renovating."

"That sounds exciting—and creepy. I bet it's helpful to have the experience of moving to a small town."

"It is."

"What brought you to Wildcat Springs from Michigan?" I asked.

"I wanted a change of scenery." Her face remained expressionless, and she pushed up her glasses.

"I see. Well, good luck with the book."

"I work diligently, so I don't need luck, Georgia Rae."

My heart flopped at her use of my middle name, and a chill traveled my spine as I left the shop.

I was almost back to my truck when I spotted the sign for Mitchell's Hardware and decided to peruse paint samples since Preston had made an excellent point about my kitchen. I shoved the remainder of my cookie in my mouth, brushed the crumbs from my hands, and entered the store.

Harry Mitchell, the grizzled owner, was sitting in his usual perch behind the counter and grunted in my direction.

"I'm looking for paint swatches," I said as if he'd haul himself off his stool and help me.

"Down that aisle." He pointed. "Back in the corner. Let me know if you need anything." He coughed and wheezed into his hanky.

Before I made it to the paint swatches, Diana Graham darted

in front of me and blocked my path. She wore a red, one-shoulder jumpsuit, which felt out of place in a hardware store.

"Pastor Jim *raved* about your turn as the church pianist." She tapped my arm a little too hard to be considered playful. "You might put me out of a job."

Not again. "I don't want to put anyone—"

"I know." She narrowed her eyes. "I'd *never* let that happen."

Yikes. Maybe she was the Cow-Heart Creeper. *Time for fishing expedition—part two.* "Did you meet the work deadline you were worried about?"

"I *always* meet deadlines," Diana said. "But it was close to midnight last evening before I was finished because of backordered office cabinets that didn't come in until late Saturday afternoon." She heaved a sigh.

As long as she was telling the truth, the last thing on her mind would've been playing a prank on me. "It was nice to see you." I attempted to step around her, but she didn't budge.

"I'll keep you on my list of substitute pianists—but don't get too comfortable." The cold intensity of her gaze reminded me of Arden.

Should I mention Arden and the piano? If I suggested another person, hopefully Diana wouldn't think I intended to dethrone her. "Arden Tanner plays the piano—if you ever need another substitute. I think she was hoping you'd ask her."

Diana waved a hand. "Oh, I'm aware. I don't suppose she told you I *did* ask her once when I was filling in for the organist, so we needed someone on piano. She panicked in the middle of 'Blessed Assurance' and scurried out. When I asked her what happened, she couldn't give me a reason. She's a strange one." Diana glanced over her shoulder. "Don't go spreading that around. I don't want to gossip."

Riiiiight. "I won't." Making a mental note to ask Cal about that incident, I slipped around Diana and finally reached the paint samples.

"What are you painting?" Diana hovered at my elbow.

Could this woman not take a hint? "My kitchen could use some sprucing up." I selected a couple of swatches in the blue and green families. "People keep telling me it's time for a change because it's not been updated since my parents remodeled in the 1980s."

"Then you need a full renovation—not a paint job." She withdrew a business card from her purse and handed it to me. "You should have a professional help with the design, and *I'm* the best around. So is my construction crew. Now that I'm finished with the offices at the Richardville airport, I have some openings in my schedule. Give me a call, and we'll chat about your budget and must-haves."

I glanced at the card. *Diana Graham Designs.* I dropped the samples and her card into my handbag. "I'll keep that in mind."

Way, *way* in the back corners of my mind.

———

That night Cal and Miss Peacock joined Gus and me for dinner. The elder Miss Peacock had little tolerance for Gus's antics, but they always sniffed each other in greeting and were content to leave each other alone. Cal and I ate leftover chicken spaghetti and a salad that I'd purchased and dumped into a bowl.

While we cleaned up, I told him what I'd learned at Pastry Delight and Mitchell's Hardware. "Diana's odd, but Arden gives me the heebie-jeebies. I mean, did you notice how she was wearing a Rangers baseball cap last night, and in Sunday school she said she'd read about your cases?" I scrubbed the casserole dish. "And we all heard her snarky comments about me."

"That was a side of her I hadn't seen before," he said. "But she did give you a backhanded compliment."

Life Lesson #7 Men can be clueless wonders.

I gave my eyes strict orders not to roll. "What if she's obsessed with you, thinks I'm in the way, and is planning to take me out because she's heartbroken over losing a chance with you?"

He wiped off the kitchen table. "Or she's a baseball fan, and she's already told us she's writing a mystery novel. She did touch base with Vanessa today and wants to go on a ride-along."

"She could be hoping to see you." Then, I remembered something else from the night before. "Did you notice how Hamlet looked funny when he realized Arden was here, and when she saw him, she seemed uncomfortable?"

"No. I was too busy trying to stop myself from slamming my fist into Wolfe's smarmy face."

I giggled at the satisfying mental image of Cal putting Wolfe flat on his back. "What if Arden's upset because she asked Hamlet out on a date, and he said *no?* Maybe she thinks he's hung up on me—not that he is. If she thought she lost out with both you *and* Hamlet because of me, that would explain her rude comment." I rinsed the casserole dish and handed it to Cal.

"Could be, but Arden seems more like the type to embarrass you instead of playing a prank on you." He dried the dish and put it away. "Is she a bit odd? Yes. But that's not a crime, and I'm far more worried about another remote possibility."

"What?"

He hung the towel on the stove. "I didn't want to worry you with this, but it's not fair to keep my concerns from you."

As glad as I was that he'd learned not to keep secrets from me, I still wasn't following. "What concerns?"

"That the beef heart isn't a stupid prank, and the person who killed Natalie Thrailkill is coming after you."

CHAPTER FIVE

I sat with a thud. No wonder Cal had insisted on searching the box for prints. Why hadn't I thought of that scenario sooner? Was it because my head was in the clouds over reuniting with him?

After Natalie had been murdered, her husband Mason had received a note that read, *How does it feel? You killed the person I loved. And now I've taken the one you love.* At the time, Cal worried I might be in danger, because he'd worked a murder case with Mason that they believed could be linked to the note.

When Cal refused to tell me what was bothering him, I broke up with him and hadn't learned about Natalie—or the note—until Cal's mom visited. Yvonne told me about the case where a murder suspect had been falsely accused and proven innocent after dying. Then I recalled another detail she had shared.

The falsely accused suspect had died of a heart attack.

Could the beef heart be a symbolic opening shot from that person's friend or relative who was now seeking revenge on Cal?

Or were Cal's old fears causing us both to overreact?

"Are you okay? You're pale." Cal knelt beside me and rubbed my back.

"What if the heart is symbolic?" My voice wobbled. "Tell me about the case you worked with Mason where the murder suspect died of a heart attack before you found evidence to exonerate him —or her."

"How'd you know about that?"

"Your mom told me."

He raked his hands through his hair. "I absolutely hate how Mason and I got the wrong guy. I've asked myself over and over what we could've done differently." He sat in the chair across from me and folded his hands. "Three years ago, a thirty-five-year old named Anita Halvorson was strangled with her Maltipoo's leash in her backyard in the middle of the night."

I shivered. "That makes me never want to take Gus out at night ever again."

"I hear you." He sighed. "Anita had recently broken up with a man named Chuck Richman. We thought he'd been stalking her, because his fingerprints were on her sliding door, we found recordings of Anita on his computer, and we uncovered the burn phone that he'd used to send threatening text messages. He didn't have an alibi for the time of her murder, so we arrested him."

"Sounds reasonable."

"We thought so. But Chuck claimed the burn phone wasn't his, and he hadn't put a hidden camera in Anita's house. He admitted his prints were on her sliding door because he missed the dog and went to see him when Anita was at work. He pleaded not guilty and died before his trial. Several months later, I discovered new evidence that pointed to Chuck's neighbor and realized he'd killed Anita and framed Chuck."

My mind swirled with the details. "Is the real Dog Leash Killer still in prison?"

"He committed suicide."

"And the police think one of Chuck's family members or friends is seeking revenge against you and Mason and started by killing Natalie?"

"According to what Mason's told me, that's the prevailing theory. Chuck's parents are dead. His close friends all checked out, and his only cousin, Travis, was living in Florida at the time of Natalie's death. Chuck's sister, who has an alibi, told the detectives she suspects his ex-girlfriend Emily Smith. She was obsessed with him, but Chuck wanted nothing to do with her. She disappeared around the time of Natalie's murder, and the police haven't been able to find her."

I stiffened. "Do you know what Emily looks like?"

"No. Why?"

"What if Emily became Arden Tanner from Michigan and moved here to torment us?"

"Then she's stupid for wanting to go on a ride-along, because we'll have to do a criminal history report as part of her application, and Vanessa made that clear. But I've seen criminals do some dumb things." He motioned toward my laptop sitting on the table. "Let's do a search to see if the police released a photo of Emily."

I opened the computer and searched for *Emily Smith Natalie Thrailkill murder*. We found an article on a local news channel's website that stated Emily Smith was wanted for questioning in connection with the murder investigation, and there was a photo of her. I squinted at the picture. "Her hair's longer than Arden's, and she's blonder. But their face shape is similar, and Emily's nose is wider. What if Emily got plastic surgery and changed her hair?" As I said the words aloud, I realized how far-fetched they sounded.

To Cal's credit, he didn't laugh. "Surgery takes money, and getting a new ID isn't as easy as the movies make it seem." He squinted at the picture. "Sweetie, I don't think Arden is Emily."

"I'm still going to do an online search for Arden."

"Go for it."

I was fairly certain I saw a flicker of amusement in his eyes, but when the only Arden Tanners I found weren't the one we knew, his expression grew serious.

"It's strange Arden doesn't have any social media accounts," Cal said. "But some people like their privacy, and that's not a crime."

I closed my laptop. "You're right." I planned to keep an eye on Arden but considered a different angle. "Did anyone play pranks on Natalie before she died?"

"Not that I'm aware of."

I looked Cal straight in the eyes. "So what happened to Natalie and Mason may not even involve you—and we're worrying and suspecting Arden for nothing?"

"Right. Mason served in Afghanistan dismantling IEDs before he became a cop. For all we know, someone from that part of his life could've been out for retribution, and we're on the wrong track with the revenge for Chuck Richman theory. It could even be another case Mason worked." He took my hand. "I just didn't want to keep my thoughts from you. Please don't worry."

His words should've been reassuring—but the apprehension in his gorgeous blue eyes told me his head didn't agree with his gut. "Okay."

"I'd better be getting home." He stood and drew me into his arms. "We'll get to the bottom of this. I promise."

His lips met mine, and I let myself forget the day's uncertainty.

The next morning, I met Brandi and Ashley for breakfast at Velda's Café in Wildcat Springs. The Tuesday special was a vegetable quiche that I wasn't too sure about, but my friends coaxed me to try. It wasn't half bad once I picked out the asparagus.

"I have some news," Brandi said after she finished showing us pictures from her trip to Europe. "Yesterday, the superintendent asked me to take the principal's job because the person he hired quit at the last minute to take a position at a school that pays more."

"That's great, hon," Ashley said. "Right?"

"I'm honored that Dr. Garcia wants me to take a leadership role, but I'm afraid I'll miss teaching." She nudged a piece of crust with her fork. "And school starts next week."

"Plus, you're not sure you want the hassle?" Even though my time in the classroom had been limited to student teaching, I had a sense about the trials a principal faced.

"Exactly," Brandi said. "The assistant principal doesn't want the job because he's close to retiring. I have my administrative license, and Dr. Garcia thinks I'd be a perfect fit—even though I've never done the job."

"You've prayed about it, right?" I asked.

"Yes, but God hasn't shown me what he wants yet. Or he has, and I'm not getting the message."

"He'll make it clear, hon," Ashley said. "You taught me that yourself."

Prayer was one area where Brandi set a good example for all of us, because she believed it was the best solution for every difficult situation. Though I'd had many moments of doubt, I knew she was right.

"I know." The turmoil churned in Brandi's eyes. "But he needs to hurry because we're on a time crunch."

"Let's pray right now," I said.

Even though I wasn't the greatest at praying aloud, I'd been trying to get over my hang up, so I led a prayer for God to show Brandi his will.

"Let's talk about something more lighthearted," Brandi said when I finished.

"I have just the thing," Ashley said. "I mentioned this to Georgia on Saturday, but could I convince you to work my booth at the arts fair on Saturday? I'm hoping to get the word out about my business."

"I'd be happy to," Brandi said.

"Yay!" Ashley smiled. "I'm sorry I'm so needy lately. Help me with my new business. Be my bridesmaids."

"That's what we're here for," Brandi said.

"Absolutely." I drained my remaining coffee. I still hadn't told them about the heart and was wondering if I should worry them. Having their insight could be helpful, so I decided to blaze ahead.

"Sorry to get away from the lighthearted topics, but I had a little incident on Sunday afternoon before small group." While they stared at me with a mix of curiosity and disgust, I explained how I'd found the heart on my porch after church and how Preston and Austin had come to my rescue and nicknamed the culprit Cow-Heart Creeper.

"The note that came with the box said, 'A dead heart for Georgia Rae, the Heartbreaker.'"

Brandi's eyes grew wide, and a worried look settled on Ashley's face.

"Any ideas who'd have it out for me?" I wanted to see who they'd guess before I told them my suspicions.

"I sure do." Brandi crossed her arms. "This morning, I woke up early, so I went to work in my classroom on a presentation I'm giving tomorrow at the tech conference we're hosting. As I was leaving to come here, I saw several students because teams are already practicing for fall sports."

I leaned forward. "And?" I sounded a bit testy, but she was going around the barn to get to the horse.

"I overheard some boys say *cow heart*."

"What?" Ashley and I said in unison.

"I know. Not exactly normal teenage conversation, right?"

"Definitely not." Had word gotten out about what'd happened to me? Or were the boys talking about it because they knew who was responsible? "Please, *please* tell me you recognized the boys."

"Yep. But the one you should talk to is Holden Miller."

CHAPTER SIX

"The heart seems like a stunt a teenage boy might pull. Especially one as ornery as Holden." I sat back in my chair. "If he *is* the Cow-Heart Creeper, it'd be such a huge relief. Cal's been worried there's a connection to Natalie Thrailkill's murderer." I briefly explained that situation. "However, I don't think that solution makes the most sense, since no one played pranks on Natalie before she died."

Ashley rubbed her bare arms. "I hope not, hon."

"No kidding," Brandi said. "I'll be happy to go with you when you talk to Holden."

I stood and removed my purse from the chair back. "How about now?"

Ashley had to get to her studio for a class, but Brandi and I walked to Latte Conspiracies. When we arrived, Bobbi Sue was wiping off tables.

"Is Holden here?" Brandi asked after Bobbi Sue greeted us.

"In the back. He stopped by for a smoothie after tennis practice." She tossed the rag on her shoulder and looked at Brandi. "What'd he do now?"

"We don't know that he did anything, but he might have helpful information," she said before explaining about the prank and what she'd overheard in the hallway. "After Georgia told me about what happened, I thought it was a strange coincidence—"

"He'd better not have anything to do with this, or I'll tan his hide." Bobbi Sue's mouth flattened, and she motioned us to an empty table before stomping into the back room. She reappeared with her teenage son in tow and steered him into a chair. "You're going to tell the whole truth and nothing but the truth, understand? If I find out you lied, you're going to be without that precious phone of yours for three full months, got it?"

"Yes." His leg bounced so much I thought he was going to blast off and rocket through the ceiling.

"What do you know about a beef heart that found its way to my porch on Sunday?" I took out my phone and showed him the picture I'd taken of the box and the heart.

Holden's leg jiggling stopped. "I did it."

Relief washed over me, and I hadn't realized how worried I'd been.

"Why?" Bobbi Sue demanded.

He squirmed. "Saturday afternoon, Blake and I were playing tennis, and he was complaining about his mom making beef heart for supper the night before. I told him how disgusting that was. But I remembered seeing one in *our* freezer when I was looking for the Klondike bars. When I said so, Blake told me I should get rid of it and was all like, 'That'd be an awesome thing to prank somebody with. Like a girl who ripped your heart out.'"

"You didn't have a girl you wanted to get back at for yourself, so you chose me since Hamlet and I broke up?" I asked.

"I heard you say you were dating Detective Perkins earlier

that day, so I told Blake about you and my brother breaking up, and now he's moving to Chicago when *The Music Man* finishes its run." He ducked his head. "We talked about what the note should say, and Blake said he'd give me a hundred bucks if I actually did it." He looked up. "His parents are loaded, so he throws money around all the time."

Bobbi Sue put her hands on her hips. "Do I not pay well enough that you have to resort to criminal behavior?"

"It was a hundred bucks, Mom."

"So you'd sell your soul to the devil for one hundred dollars. Good to know that's your price."

"I haven't spent it," he said.

"And you won't. You're going to donate every penny to our church." Bobbi Sue rolled her eyes. "Go on. Tell Georgia the rest of your sordid tale."

I fought a grin.

"After my parents left for the early church service, I put on the gloves Mom uses for the dishes, found the heart in our freezer, and stuck it in a cardboard box. I even used some of my sister's old pink stickers to decorate the box. I thought if it looked girly, no one would suspect me."

"You're a true criminal mastermind." Bobbi Sue snorted.

I unsuccessfully choked back a laugh, but Brandi managed to keep a straight face, which boded well for her possible future as a high school principal.

Holden's face reddened. "I delivered it when I knew you'd be at church, but your dog must've sensed something was wrong, because he was barking like crazy the whole time I was there." He studied his hands. "I'm sorry. I was mad because I don't want Hamlet to move, and if you guys had stayed together maybe. . ."

Like mother, like son.

"I've negatively influenced you." Bobbi Sue looked at Brandi and me. "I've struggled with Hamlet's decisions myself and wouldn't shut up about it—"

"No, Mom. I'm responsible for my own choices."

She folded her arms over her chest. "Oh, I know. You're *absolutely* going to be held responsible. I'm just saying I shouldn't have been so negative." Bobbi Sue wiggled her fingers. "Hand over your phone."

Holden obeyed.

Bobbi Sue turned to me. "How can Holden make this up to you?"

For a second, I thought about putting him to work in my garden but figured he'd suffer enough being apart from his precious phone. "Donate the money to your church and stay out of any more trouble." I stood and patted him on the shoulder. "I forgive you."

On the way home, I called Cal. "Good news," I said as soon as he answered. "I found the Cow-Heart Creeper."

When I told him about Holden, he laughed. "I'm glad it was an ornery teenage boy and not . . . you know."

"I feel the same way. I'm so relieved I can't even be mad."

"I would've loved to have seen Bobbi Sue's face."

"It was priceless. She called him a 'criminal mastermind.'"

He chuckled. "Hey, I've got to get back to work, but I can't wait to see you tonight. I'll bring dinner."

"Perfect. I love you."

"Love you too."

I disconnected and turned into my driveway. As soon as I parked in the garage, I heard Gus barking frantically. He must've slurped a lot of water this morning and needed to go outside.

I rushed inside, entered my passcode on the security system

keypad next to the back door, and stepped into the utility room where Gus was whining and rattling his crate. I released him, and he tore into my kitchen with a ferocious bark. Clutching my phone, I followed and caught a whiff of vinegar in the air.

A strangled gasp slipped from my mouth.

Large patches of my kitchen's flower-basket wallpaper had been stripped from the walls, but not a single scrap remained on the floor—or anywhere else. On the wall above the table someone had scrawled a poem in red marker, and my heart dropped as I read the words.

A mystery for Georgia Rae.
Who'll jump right into the fray.
Heartbreak can be cruel.
You feel like a fool.
So it's time for a change today.

CHAPTER SEVEN

I moved forward in slow motion while my pulse pummeled my neck. Holden had admitted to being the Cow-Heart Creeper, but he wouldn't do something this destructive—or poetic —would he?

No. He'd been at tennis practice, Brandi had seen him at the school, and I'd finished talking to him less than fifteen minutes ago.

How had someone disarmed my security system? I hadn't forgotten to set it because I'd just entered the code. With shaky fingers, I tapped Cal's number on my phone, but the call went straight to voicemail.

"I got home, and Gus was going crazy and . . ." I drew a wobbly breath. "Somebody came into my kitchen and tore off my wallpaper and wrote a limerick on the wall in red marker, and I don't know what to do, so please, I need you to tell me what to do." I disconnected and prayed my babbling message had made sense.

As I snapped pictures of the kitchen, I realized I couldn't stay here. For all I knew, the culprit could be hiding in the house. By the time I called 9-1-1 and someone from the sheriff's department arrived, the boogeyman—or woman—could make short work of me.

"Gus!"

Panting, he scampered back into the kitchen.

"Let's go, buddy." I fastened his leash, reset the security system, and locked the door behind me. We leaped into the truck, and the tires kicked up gravel as the truck skidded out of the driveway.

I had no idea where I was going, and when my phone connected to the sound system and the choir's song blasted through the speakers, I jabbed the volume button. I couldn't handle the noise right now. Not even choral music could soothe me.

The silence helped me gather my thoughts, and I headed for the sheriff's department in Richardville. If Cal wasn't there, Vanessa could help. In the meantime, I needed to confirm Holden's whereabouts. I tapped the voice command button on my steering wheel. "Call Evan Beckworth cell."

"Calling Evan Beckworth on cell," the computerized voice said.

My friend was the varsity tennis coach and would be able to tell me if Holden was at practice—the entire time.

"Georgia! I was getting ready to text you. You're a mind reader."

"Did Holden Miller or his friend Blake leave tennis practice early today?" I blurted.

"That's random. Why?"

"Please just answer the question! I wouldn't be asking you if it weren't important." I punched the brakes and screeched to a stop at an intersection.

"No, they were there the whole time—from seven until nine.

In fact, Blake and another kid stayed after practice and played a challenge match. Did they do something wrong?"

I gripped the steering wheel and zoomed through the intersection. "No. They couldn't have." There wouldn't have been time for Holden to strip my wallpaper and make it back to Latte Conspiracies. "I'm sorry to be so frantic, but Holden has played a harmless prank on me in the past, and Blake was in on it." I didn't want to get the boys in trouble with their coach, but if I didn't say enough, Evan would go into guidance counselor mode and coax the information out of me. "Then today, someone stripped my kitchen wallpaper and wrote a limerick on the wall while I was at breakfast with Brandi and Ashley, and I'm ruling them out."

"What? That's . . . sick. Are you all right?"

His caring tone reminded me why I'd had a crush on him for years before I met Cal. "Yes." If I told myself that enough times, I'd believe it.

Right?

"Are you helping Cal with a case?"

"No." I didn't want to answer any more questions. Time for a distraction move. "Why were you going to text me?"

He hesitated, as if he didn't want to drop the previous subject but thought better of it. "Since Kelsey's coming home, I want to have a get together for our friends. Ashley said I could rent her studio space. Are you and Cal free a week from Saturday at seven?"

In my current mental state, it was hard to care about a party. "I'll double check with Cal, but you can tentatively count us in." Kelsey was Cal's cousin who'd been working as a nurse at a clinic in Ethiopia.

"Sounds good. And Georgia?"

"Yes?"

"Please be careful."

"I will." I disconnected, turned off the county road onto the highway that led to Richardville, and considered another possibility about my wallpaper.

Had Austin and Preston decided to prank me, and I was freaking out for no reason?

A while ago, they'd made a key to my house with that intention, though they'd never followed through. I found out they had the key when they stayed with me earlier this year along with their sister Makayla. After their visit, I hadn't taken the key, but I *had* changed my alarm system's code and hadn't given them the new one.

Mom and Dan had the new code. Had they written it down and the twins found it? That was entirely possible, because Mom had trouble remembering passwords. Preston had teased me about renovating my kitchen yesterday, had *specifically mentioned* getting rid of the wallpaper, and they both knew that Holden's note called me a heartbreaker. Their sister Makayla might even be in on the joke, because she was a poet. She was working at a church camp for the summer, but her brothers could've easily contacted her.

That had to be it. It was Pick on Georgia Week, and Presty, Austy, and Mak had joined in on the juvenile fun.

I gritted my teeth.

Forget the sheriff's department. I was going to pay the twin idiots a visit first. I kept my eyes on the road. They had no right to play a trick like this. Even if they intended to help me paint my kitchen, this joke was thoughtless. I kneaded the steering wheel while Gus, who hadn't stopped panting, wiggled on the seat beside me. The passenger window was streaked with his nose prints.

I hurried across Richardville to the Winters Group where Preston and Austin worked. One of them had better be there because I wasn't above tracking them down while they were showing clients houses.

I eased into the parking lot in front of the brick building and stopped beside Austin's Jeep. Across the lot, Preston's Mustang was parked in the shade of a silver maple. Since the weather was breezy, I left the windows partially open for Gus and marched inside.

This would be quick.

A pretty young woman with wavy brown hair greeted me from behind a reception desk that displayed the company's logo and was trimmed with weathered wood.

"I need to see Preston and Austin Farthing. Are they here?"

"Yes." Her friendly expression faded as she stood. "May I ask what this is about?"

"Tell them their stepsister is here, and they'd better hustle their butts out here!"

"Right away." With her hair swishing, she bolted out of her seat and around a corner.

I must've scared her, because she could've just called them.

A minute later she hurried back. "They'll be with you momentarily. May I get you something to drink?"

"No. Thank you."

"Please have a seat." She motioned to a gray couch and two armchairs arranged in front of a stone fireplace that stretched to the vaulted ceiling.

I stalked toward the couch but couldn't bring myself to sit. Instead, I paced in front of the picture window. Gus had stuck his head out of the truck and was sniffing the air.

"Georgia?" Preston darted into the reception area. "What's going on?"

Austin appeared behind him. "Jenna said it's urgent."

"Could we step outside? Gus is with me, and I'd like to keep an eye on him."

"No problem." Preston exchanged a worried look with Austin.

I pushed out the door, stopped next to my truck, and took a deep breath. "Be completely straight with me." I tugged my braid. "Did you strip some of the wallpaper in my kitchen this morning and have Makayla write a creepy limerick? Because if you did, we'll have a big laugh and you can help me pick out a paint color, and I won't hold a grudge. I just need to know you guys are responsible—"

"It wasn't us." Austin shaded his eyes. "I swear."

I'd never seen him so serious, and if he was faking the shock on his face, he deserved an Oscar.

"No way." Preston shifted and appeared equally horrified. "I teased you about needing to get rid of the wallpaper, but that's all it was." He held up both hands. "I swear. I have more respect for you than that."

"Same here. Even if we like giving you a hard time." Austin said. "When did this happen?"

"This morning. Sometime after eight. I had breakfast with Brandi and Ashley in Wildcat Springs, went to Latte Conspiracies, and got home a little before ten." I held out my phone and swiped through the pictures.

"I'm sorry somebody did this, but we've been here all morning. You can ask our boss and a bunch of other people." Austin motioned toward the building.

A wave a dizziness passed over me, and I leaned against my truck for support as the breeze swirled around us. What if Cal's theory was right?

"She's super pale, Austin." Preston looped his arm around my elbow. "Get the dog out and meet us inside."

I held out my key, and Austin took it, and then Preston led me into the building while the receptionist watched from the front desk.

"Jenna, grab Georgia a water bottle, please," Preston said.

She hopped up while he guided me past a large workspace

with at least a dozen desks. We entered a glass-walled conference room where he rolled out a white leather chair and motioned for me to sit at the table.

A woman wearing purple-framed glasses appeared in the doorway. "Is something wrong? I thought I heard commotion."

Preston introduced her as Barb Winters, the agency's owner. "Will you confirm what time Austin and I got here this morning?"

"It was before eight because you were both here when I arrived." Barb looked at me. "They're real go-getters, so it's not unusual for them to be here early."

"And you never saw us leave?" Preston asked.

"No. Why all the questions?"

"Someone played a prank on me this morning, and I thought my stepbrothers might've done it, but clearly, they didn't." I had met Brandi and Ashley at eight. "I was hoping they did because there'd be a simple explanation."

"I see. I hope you figure it out." She took a step backward. "I'll be in my office if you need me."

Jenna brought the water bottle and then slipped out. I cracked open the lid and took a sip. "I'm sorry I accused you and—"

"Don't be." Preston sat next to me. "It'd be better if we'd done it because we'd know you weren't in danger. Seems like the Cow-Heart Creeper is escalating."

"No. I figured out the Cow-Heart Creeper's identity this morning." I told him about Holden and how he couldn't have stripped my wallpaper. "And to think I was relieved the heart wasn't a sign of something more serious to come."

"It's a super weird coincidence that two different people played pranks on you in such a short time span," Preston said.

"I know." Goosebumps peppered my arms. "Whoever

stripped the wallpaper must've known what Holden did, because the message on the wall called me a heartbreaker."

"Let me see that poem again."

I handed over my phone, and he studied the pictures. "'A mystery for Georgia Rae. Who'll jump right into the fray.' This person knows you can't help trying to solve any case that comes along," he said.

"The last line feels threatening too."

"For sure. I thought limericks were supposed to be funny, but this one definitely isn't."

Austin and Gus entered the conference room. "He did his business," Austin said. "Just number one." He handed Gus's leash to me.

"Is Barb cool with Gus being here?" I asked.

Austin joined us at the table. "She brings her Pomeranian all the time and gave Gus a pat when we came in."

"Georgia found the Cow-Heart Creeper." Preston returned my phone and updated Austin.

"Awesomesauce," Austin said. "What's the plan for catching the Wallpaper Bandit?"

"I'm waiting to hear from Cal." I took another drink and stroked Gus's head. "This incident is much more serious since it involves vandalism."

"And breaking and entering," Austin said.

"Nothing was broken, so whoever got in had a key." I groaned. "It had to be the one hidden under the welcome mat on my back porch."

Life Lesson #188: A hidden key under a welcome mat is a gift to your friendly neighborhood vandal.

"Not good," Preston said.

"What were you thinking, sissy?" Austin shook his head.

"It was stupid. I know, but someone also had to have my security code to get in."

Preston rested his elbows on the table and appeared thoughtful. "Your security system has open and close reporting, right?"

"What's that?"

"An account of what code was used to disarm and arm the system. We use it here, so Barb knows who's been in and out," Preston said. "Dad and Jill have it at their house, so I bet you do too since Dad bought you the same model and service they have."

"That sounds familiar," I said. "Did I have to give the company my email to get reports?"

"Yes," Preston said. "But if you're the only one coming and going, I see why you never got around to it. You could call the company and see if they can tell you what time the system was disarmed and what code was used."

"I only have one code." I'd never thought about creating more than one, but I should have. Then it might've been easier to figure out the breach. However, it wouldn't have stopped someone with evil intent.

"Check," Preston said. "In case an old code is still active."

"You're a good sidekick."

"I know." He winked.

"Hey? What about me? I took your dog out," Austin said. "Don't I get any credit?"

"You're great too." While I appreciated their attempts to lighten the mood, I didn't even feel like rolling my eyes at their silliness.

Instead, I dialed the number for Safe Home and navigated through an automated menu. When I finally contacted an actual person, I explained the situation to Joan—without mentioning the wallpaper.

Keyboard clicks sounded over the line. "Ms. Winston, according to the open and close report for your system, someone disarmed it at 8:32 this morning and armed it at 9:24."

I froze.

"Then, it was disarmed again at 10:03 and armed at 10:08."

That time was me. "What passcode was used?"

She told me, and it was my newest one—both times. My stomach tightened.

"If you have any more questions, my extension is 3081. Have a safe and secure day." Joan disconnected, and I dropped my phone into my lap and recapped the conversation for the twins.

"So the question is, who has your code?" Austin said. "Because I'm going to go out on a limb and say she changed it after we stayed with her, Presty."

"Dude, that's not going out on a limb."

"You're right." I managed a half smile. "Mom, Dan, Grandpa, Brandi, and Ashley are the only ones with the new code."

"Why not Cal?" Austin asked.

"We just started dating again, and I hadn't thought about it."

Preston leaned back and crossed his arms. "Are you certain Hamlet never saw you enter the code?"

"No." I hadn't tried to hide it from him, but I'd never shared the code because there'd never been a reason for him to enter my house when I wasn't home. Maybe Hamlet knew Holden left the beef heart and had called me a heartbreaker and decided to take the prank to another level. I pushed the disloyal thoughts away.

"How'd you share the code?" Austin asked. "Like did you email or something?"

"You think someone could've hacked her account?" Preston said.

Austin nodded. "It's a possibility."

"I told people in person." At least I thought so, but right now, I was having trouble keeping my thoughts straight.

"Did they write it down?" Preston asked.

"Mom did, which is how I thought you guys figured it out."

The guys exchanged glances.

"I don't like this," Preston said.

"Same here, dude."

I squeezed the bridge of my nose. "Guys, there's something else you need to know." I told them Cal was concerned that one of Chuck Richman's loved ones might be out to kill me—like Natalie Thrailkill—and about my fears that Arden might be Chuck's ex-girlfriend Emily. "But that seems farfetched, and no one played pranks on Natalie before she died."

"Super creepy limerick called you a heartbreaker," Austin said. "If the Wallpaper Bandit is Natalie's killer, why say that when Cal's the one who'd be heartbroken . . . if you died?"

"I concur, bro. We should look at the same people who were our Cow-Heart Creeper suspects," Preston said.

I hoped they were right. "Whoever vandalized my kitchen had to be available between 8:32 and 9:24 this morning. Taryn Anderson has been on vacation with her family, but she's not due back until Wednesday, so I doubt she has anything to do with this."

"That's good," Austin said. "I'd hate to think hot baker chick is a psychopath."

Of all things to focus on. "Arden Tanner may not be Emily Smith in disguise, but she definitely doesn't like me. She's an aspiring mystery novelist, so maybe she thought writing a poem would be more dramatic than just a regular old threat."

"Yeah." Preston looked at my phone again. "The limerick is a weird choice, so it must be significant."

"Possibly." As I patted Gus's head, I thought of something else. "Arden works at Pastry Delight, so if she's covering for Taryn, she *couldn't* have been at my house this morning. I don't know how Arden would've known to call me a heartbreaker unless she heard about the beef heart prank."

"Aren't you always complaining people in your town know your business before you do?" Preston asked. "Word probably got out."

"True. Wolfe Sommers works at Latte Conspiracies and could've heard about the beef heart prank from Holden. Plus, I was in the shop this morning, and Wolfe wasn't there so—"

"Time out." Preston made the signal. "How would Arden and Wolfe know about your outdated wallpaper?"

"Well . . . they were both at my house on Sunday." I told them about small group.

"You let those crazies in your house!" Austin gaped at me. "Sissy . . . What were you thinking?"

Now he sounded like their dad too. "I was trying to be hospitable." My friends hadn't exactly given me a choice when they'd arrived with guests in tow.

"What if Wolfe and Arden are working together?" Austin said. "She wrote the poem, and he's the vandal."

"Possibly." I chewed my lip. Could Arden's disdain for Wolfe have been an act? Ashley thought so.

"Have you mentioned the kitchen renovation to anyone else?" Preston asked.

I froze. "Yesterday, I thought about your suggestion that I should paint, and while I was at the hardware store looking at samples, I ran into Diana Graham—she's an interior designer and plays the piano at Cal's church. She said I should do more than paint and gave me her card. Plus, I used the words 'time for a change' when I was talking to her."

"How would she know to call you a heartbreaker?" Austin asked.

"I saw her Saturday at Latte Conspiracies, and she heard me turn down Wolfe's offer of a date. Wait—no." I considered Diana's tennis attire, and how she hadn't looked the least bit disheveled from the heat. "Diana was wearing a tennis dress, and Holden told me that he and his buddy Blake planned the beef heart prank while they were playing tennis on Saturday afternoon. She might've overheard them talking. But why would she use that information to hurt me?"

The Twin Menaces exchanged glances.

"She's crazy and needs a new client," Preston said.

"Or she has a thing for Cal, wants you out of the picture, and is messing with your head before . . ." Austin drew his finger in a slashing motion across his throat.

Preston elbowed him. "Knock it off."

We fell silent, and then my phone chimed. "That's Cal. I'll see what he says."

"We'll give you some privacy," Preston said, and the guys exited, closing the glass door behind them.

"Are you okay?" Cal asked.

"I will be. Gus will too. He's with me."

"Good. Why didn't you call 9-1-1?"

"I was too freaked to wait for a sheriff's deputy to get there."

"Fair enough. Where are you now?"

"Preston and Austin's real estate office. I was on my way to the sheriff's department when I thought they might've been responsible, so I detoured. But they weren't, and they have alibis." I lowered my voice and glanced at the door. "I hate to admit this, but I hoped they were guilty."

"That would be easier for all of us. Did you have your security system on?"

"Yes. But I was stupid and had a key under my welcome mat."

"Oh, Georgia." He groaned.

"I know, I know. That was stupid." I told him I'd ruled out Holden Miller and his friend Blake and about my call to the security system company and the time the Wallpaper Bandit had been in my house. I also shared my suspicions about Diana Graham.

"Good work. I'll swing by their office to check on you and to get your key in case the one under your mat is missing. Your kitchen's a crime scene, so why don't you see if the twins will take you and Gus to lunch while I'm looking for evidence in your kitchen."

"Okay." My voice wobbled.

"We'll figure this out. I love you."

"I love you too." Tears pricked my eyes as I disconnected. Why was God letting someone torture me now that Cal and I were finally happy?

CHAPTER EIGHT

After Cal stopped by the real estate office, Austin and Preston escorted Gus and me to William's Home Supply where I purchased new locks and a video doorbell. Then, we returned to Wildcat Springs where we went to Pizza Heaven because of the pet-friendly patio seating.

"Where are we going to investigate after we eat?" Preston asked as soon as the hostess seated us at an out-of-the-way table under the shade of a blue umbrella.

I looped Gus's leash around my chair, and he sprawled under the table and rested his head on his paws. "We'll get dessert at Pastry Delight and possibly coffee at Latte Conspiracies." These seemed like harmless activities.

Preston grabbed a breadstick from the basket. "I knew it."

"I love being your sidekick," Austin said.

"We're your bodyguards too," Preston added. "By the way, we'll be staying with you again. Right, Austy?"

"Yep."

"You guys don't have to do that. Cal lives down the road, and—"

"We insist," Austin said. "You know what'll happen if you don't let us."

I knew. Oh, how I knew, and he wasn't talking about the Wallpaper Bandit striking again.

"Do you really want to live with Jill and Dan Lovebird?" Preston asked.

"No. No, I do not." Our parents had been married for almost six years, but they still acted like newlyweds more often than their children wanted to see.

The twins tapped their breadsticks together. "Roomies again!"

Jesus, help. Shaking my head, I picked up a menu.

Just then, the hostess led Diana Graham across the patio. Her phone was pressed to her ear, and she wore a sleeveless black sheath dress with strappy red sandals. She walked with a slight limp that hadn't been there the last two times I'd talked to her. With a grimace, she eased into her seat and didn't appear to notice me—probably because I was sitting behind a planter of zinnias.

"Darling, I had the most *awful* morning." Diana's voice carried above the traffic noise. "I pulled a muscle on my morning run, *and* a client cancelled a huge project on me."

Had she vandalized my kitchen because she needed me to hire her? Surely not.

Diana examined a fingernail. "Then I broke a nail after I *just* had a manicure yesterday."

"Earth to Georgia," Preston said. "Do you want to share a pizza?"

"Shh. I'm trying to eavesdrop on Diana Graham," I whispered and hitched my thumb toward her table.

As if they'd choreographed the move, they covered their faces up to their eyes with their menus and watched with me.

"Subtle, guys. Really subtle."

"I honestly don't know," Diana said. "I suspect money is an issue. What else could it be? I'm the best designer around." She tittered and then listened. "Darling, I need to scoot. My day is about to get *a lot* better." She disconnected and tucked her phone into her handbag.

My jaw dropped as Wolfe Sommers strolled over to Diana's table.

"Now who's the subtle one, sissy." Austin tapped my arm. "Close your mouth before a fly buzzes in."

"That's Wolfe Sommers," I hissed.

Preston cringed. "Do you think they're on a date?"

"Isn't she too old for him?" Austin asked.

The sight of Wolfe must've been a healing balm, because Diana stood without a hint of a grimace and hugged him.

"I've heard she likes younger men." Had Wolfe hitting on me made Diana jealous? "If they're dating, I'm wondering if it's a new development. When I talked to her Saturday, she referred to him as the 'naughty barista.'"

The twins snickered.

"Stay here, and watch Gus." Before the boys could protest, I hopped up and marched over to Diana and Wolfe's table. "Hello," I said. "I've been meaning to call you, Diana."

Wolfe gave me his usual once-over while Diana regarded me with a cold stare.

"What can I do for you?" she asked.

"I've been considering what you said about doing a kitchen renovation instead of painting, and at first, I was resistant to the idea of change, but the more I think about it, the more I realize what a good idea it would be to update after all, and if I did, I'd like to consult with you about the design since I've heard such good things about your work."

While yammering, I'd been keeping a close eye on Diana's and Wolfe's reactions. Her face had softened, and Wolfe appeared much more interested in the breadstick he was devouring than my blathering.

"Excellent. Call my assistant, and make an appointment." She opened her menu.

She wasn't going to dismiss me that easily.

"I was thinking my friend Hamlet could do the renovations—"

"I only work with my own crew, and you'll have to agree to that if you hire me." Her eyes narrowed. "Besides, I wouldn't hire Hamlet Miller for *anything* construction related."

I made a valiant effort not to look like I wanted to tackle her.

"Why? He's a good dude." Wolfe snatched another breadstick and chomped off the end with animal-like ferocity.

"Hamlet should stick to acting, and that's all I'm going to say because I wouldn't want to gossip." Diana straightened her silverware. "Now, excuse us, Georgia Rae. You have my card, so give my office a call when you're ready."

I manufactured a fake smile. "Enjoy your lunch." I hurried back to our table, but I was nearly certain I felt Wolfe's gaze on me.

"Is it a date or not?" Preston whispered as I sat.

"She was eager to get rid of me, so I'd say she thinks it is, but Wolfe looks like he's here for the food," I said. "And she *really* doesn't like Hamlet." I quietly told them how Diana had insulted my friend. "She tried to make it sound like she didn't approve of his carpentry work, but I have a feeling there's more to the story." I studied Diana as she chatted with Wolfe, who was reaching for yet another breadstick.

I'd have to talk to Hamlet—soon.

When the twins and I finished our pizza, we walked down Pearl Street to Pastry Delight, but the lights were off, and the closed sign hung inside the door.

"That's weird." I cupped my hands around my face and peered through the shop window. "I've never known Taryn to close the shop for lunch, but maybe since she's gone, Arden decided to take a break."

Wanda, my step-grandmother, who'd married Grandpa Winston back in February, exited the antique store next door. "Why hello, Georgia."

"Hi, Wanda." I quickly introduced my stepbrothers. "How are you?"

"Fine, fine. I hope you aren't having a craving for cupcakes like I am." She brushed her silvery bangs aside. "I was hoping Pastry Delight would finally be open after I finished shopping, but the antique store owner told me the shop's been closed all day."

"Oh, man." Austin groaned. "I wanted a cookie."

"Me too," Preston chimed in, matching his brother whine for whine.

Amusement flickered in Wanda's eyes. "Gentlemen, I completely understand that sentiment. I suppose I'll come back tomorrow. Take care." She strolled down the street.

"If the shop's been closed all morning, then Arden wasn't working and would've had opportunity to vandalize my kitchen," I said as soon as Wanda was out of earshot.

"Or she's sick," Austin said.

"Could be. Let's see if Holden is at Latte Conspiracies. I want to ask if he saw Diana Graham playing tennis on Saturday."

As soon as we entered the coffee shop and Holden spotted us, his eyes widened. I suspected it was because the Twin Menaces were flanking me so closely that they were making a Georgia Rae Sandwich.

"Hi, Georgia." Red splotches crept up Holden's neck. "What can I get you guys?"

"Nothing for me, but I have another question about what we discussed this morning." Normally, I'd purchase a drink in exchange for information, but I was full after eating lunch and intended to milk this situation with Holden—even though I truly had forgiven him.

"Okay." Holden glanced at my stepbrothers.

"When you and Blake were planning the prank on Saturday, was there anyone else playing tennis?"

He scrunched up his face. "A couple of ladies who are regular customers—Diana Graham and her sister Arden Tanner."

CHAPTER NINE

"Plot twist," Preston and Austin whispered in sing-songy unison.

Yes. Plot twist indeed.

Funny how Diana hadn't mentioned Arden was her sister— or that Arden hadn't told me either. However, the family connection gave Arden a compelling reason to move from Michigan to Wildcat Springs and meant that Arden probably wasn't Chuck Richman's ex-girlfriend Emily Smith in disguise.

However, that didn't mean Arden wasn't out to get me for a different reason. "Could Diana and Arden have overheard you and Blake planning the prank?" I asked Holden.

"Yeah. We weren't exactly trying to be quiet." Holden looked back and forth between the twins and me. "Did they say something about us?"

"No," I said. "Unless there's more you're not telling me."

He glanced away. "No."

"You sure?" Preston asked in a voice that sounded an awful lot like his dad's.

"We'll find out if you're lying." Austin stepped closer to the counter and curled his fingers into a fist.

Holden held up both hands. "Blake and I didn't plan any more pranks. I swear."

Then what was he hiding? "Do you know why Diana Graham wouldn't want to hire Hamlet to do renovation work?"

"I don't know. Because he's moving?" Holden shrugged. "Ask him."

"Is Arden interested in dating your brother?" Preston asked.

"Do I look like I care that much about my brother's personal life?" Holden folded his arms over his chest.

"You cared enough to leave a cow heart on his ex-girlfriend's porch." Preston drilled Holden with a blistering gaze.

Holden's face reddened, and he eyed the door. "Do you want anything to drink?"

"Nope," I said. "But I have another question—and you owe me."

He huffed. "Fine."

"Did Wolfe Sommers ever hear you and Blake discussing the prank?" I asked.

"Maybe. Blake brought the hundred bucks he owed me while I was working on Monday—and Wolfe was here," Holden said. "Do I get to know why you're asking all these questions?"

"Nope," I said. "But have a good one." Preston, Austin, and I filed outside into the heat.

"He's totally lying—and it has to do with Hamlet," Preston said.

"I know," I said as we climbed into Austin's Jeep. "And I'll keep digging until I find out why."

***

When Preston, Austin, and I returned to my house, Cal met us in the driveway. Preston and Austin took Gus for a walk by my pond so Cal and I could talk privately.

"What'd you find?" I asked as we entered my kitchen.

"Whoever did this used a scoring tool and vinegar solution to loosen the wallpaper before stripping it. The scraps that were torn off were nowhere to be found, so I assume the person took them."

"I'm out of vinegar and don't have a scoring tool, which means the Wallpaper Bandit came prepared. What else?"

"The key under your doormat had prints that I'm confident will match yours, but we'll check—the same with the security system keypad and doorknob. I can't imagine that someone who was smart enough to get around your security system didn't wear gloves."

"Now what?"

"The vandal was parked in your driveway for about forty-five minutes," he said. "Someone driving by might've seen something, so I'm going to talk to people who live in the area."

"The Wallpaper Bandit could've parked behind one of my barns."

"I still want to talk to your neighbors."

I glanced at the limerick on the wall, and the words mocked me, causing me to turn away. "Let's go talk on the porch."

Cal rested his hand on my back, and we settled outside. Gus was barking at one of the ducks swimming in my pond while Preston fought to keep him from launching himself into the water.

"The twins and I saw Diana and Wolfe together at Pizza Heaven." I told him about her phone conversation and what she'd said about Hamlet.

Cal nodded.

"Pastry Delight hasn't been open all day, so if Arden *wasn't* working, then she had the opportunity to strip my wallpaper. And who knows what Diana was doing this morning—besides running and pulling a muscle."

"How would Diana or Arden know to call you a heartbreaker?" Cal asked.

I shared what we'd learned from Holden about Diana, Arden, and Wolfe.

"Now that I know Arden and Diana are sisters, I can see the family resemblance. It's funny Arden never mentioned they're related," he said. "I've never heard anyone at church talk about it either."

"But how much do you actually pay attention to your church's gossip?"

He chuckled. "Not at all."

That's what I'd thought. "Maybe they don't get along."

"Then why would they play tennis and go to the same church?"

I shook my head. "Since I don't have a sister, I'm no expert on the complexities of that kind of relationship."

"Did you happen to tell Holden about your kitchen vandalism?"

"No way. But the twins and I got the sense that he was lying to us—possibly about something involving Hamlet."

"I'll follow up with Holden later this afternoon, because even though you confirmed he couldn't have vandalized your kitchen, I want to explore the possibility he's working with someone and lied to cover for that person."

My heart somersaulted as my earlier doubts resurfaced. "Someone like Hamlet? You don't *really* think he—"

"I don't." Cal put his arm around me. "However, it's suspicious that Holden's friend Blake forked over a hundred bucks for a prank—even if his parents have a lot of money. And with the timing of back-to-back pranks, I want to confirm an adult wasn't involved."

"I can't believe this is happening." I rubbed my goosebumpy arms.

"God will take care of us." Cal kissed my forehead. "We'll get your locks changed, fix your security system code, and I'll help you install the video doorbell."

I appreciated that he wasn't trying to sugar coat this situation.

"And you're going to promise me never to put a key outside ever again."

"I promise." I should've known better.

"Whoever is doing this will make a mistake, and when that sicko does, we'll catch him—or her."

I leaned against Cal's muscular chest and tried to let his comforting words and action plan reassure me.

I couldn't quite get there.

CHAPTER TEN

B efore Cal left, we changed the code on my alarm system, and I created a special combination for Preston and Austin that was different than my primary code.

When Cal was gone, I surveyed my kitchen with Preston and Gus by my side. Austin had to show a house to a client, but Preston had insisted on staying. I hadn't even attempted to argue, which went a long way in demonstrating my frame of mind.

Preston whipped off his tie and tossed it onto the kitchen table. "We need to get rid of the creepy message before we change your locks. It won't take that long to strip the rest of the paper."

"Not in your dress clothes. Let me see if some of Dakota's old stuff is still lying around."

Preston followed me upstairs to my brother's childhood room, and after pawing through his dresser, I located an old Purdue T-shirt that looked a little small and a ratty pair of jeans. "Will this do?"

"Good thing I'm not an IU fan, or I'd have to go shirtless." He grinned as he took the clothes.

I left him to change and returned to the kitchen where I stood in the middle of the room. As much as I didn't want to admit it, Preston was right. I'd been hanging onto the past by refusing to update. Whoever had meant me harm had done me a favor. I'd put Preston to work changing the locks while I packed the kitchen.

And then we were going to have some demolition fun.

"Are you *sure* you know what you're doing?" Preston asked a few hours later as we stood in my kitchen.

We'd fixed the locks, installed the video doorbell, stripped the remaining wallpaper, and emptied all of the cabinet drawers and shelves. Preston helped me lug my kitchen table into the living room, and we dragged the appliances into the garage and plugged in the refrigerator. I'd found some old plastic sheets in the barn that I'd tacked in the opening between my kitchen and living room.

"These cabinets aren't worth saving. The countertop has seen better days, and I need to get out my frustration." I brandished a sledgehammer. "Are you with me?"

"Yeeeee-haaaww!" He leaped across the kitchen, grabbed a cabinet door, and yanked it off, tossing it aside with a maniacal victory roar. He ripped off the next door. And the next.

I wielded the sledgehammer and drove it into the island, splintering the laminate countertop. "Argh!" I swung again, breaking the remaining pieces. "Take that, Wallpaper Bandit!" I kicked in the island's side panels for good measure.

Someone knocked on my back door, and when I answered, Brandi peeked around me.

"What in the world is going on?" she asked.

She held a foil-wrapped plate, and I hoped there were

cookies hiding under the covering. It was a safe bet because she often baked—and shared with friends.

Preston dropped a cabinet door with a clatter and smoothed his hair as he approached the door. "Hey, Brandi. It's demo day."

"Okaaay." Since she was wearing flip-flops, she picked her way inside while holding up the plate. "Cookies. I was stress baking since I decided to take the principal's job."

"Congratulations," I said.

"Pray for me. My first day is tomorrow."

"What kind of cookies are those?" Preston asked.

Leave it to him to be worried about the food. But I was in no place to judge when it came to dessert consumption.

"Chewy chocolate chip." She surveyed me. "When did you decide to renovate?"

"This afternoon. You can put those in the living room."

She pushed aside the plastic and deposited the plate onto the kitchen table out of Gus's reach. "I'm confused." She looked back and forth between Preston and me.

Preston brushed his hands together. "What she's not telling you is that someone started the demolition for her while she was at breakfast this morning."

That was one way of saying it.

She put her hands on her hips. "Explain."

"Someone got into my house and stripped the wallpaper—and left this heartwarming limerick." I took my phone out of my back pocket and show her the picture I'd taken.

Her eyes widened. "That's awful. Wait. Could Holden have somehow done this?"

"Evan confirmed he was at tennis practice the whole time, so unless he's working with someone, he's innocent." I told her what I'd learned about Arden, Diana, and Wolfe.

"How did this person get in?" she asked. "Did you not set your alarm?"

"Someone used my hidden key—and knew my security code."

"You need to stay with me," Brandi said.

"I'll be fine. You have enough on your mind right now. We've changed the locks, updated the security code, and Cal's less than a half mile away."

"Austy and I are on guard duty."

She looked back and forth between Preston and me. "Fine. I wouldn't want to meet you and your brother in a dark alley."

He beamed, and underneath the tight T-shirt, he flexed his pecs. "Thanks."

"Don't be so sure that's a compliment."

Laughing, he batted the crinkly plastic aside and dove for the cookies.

"Is this a good time for a renovation?" she asked.

"Why not?"

"Do you have a dumpster? You need some place to put all this . . . debris."

Why hadn't I thought of that? *Oh. I don't know, Georgia? Maybe because some psycho is playing mind games with you?* "I'll call and rent one tomorrow. We'll just drag the trash outside and make a pile."

"Okay, then." She gazed at the mess. "How can I help?"

Before Brandi left, she helped Preston and me remove the linoleum flooring. Then, Austin brought home lasagna, salad, and breadsticks from my favorite restaurant in Richardville— Salvador's. Cal walked through the front door behind him, and they stopped in my living room and gaped at the boxes cluttering the space.

"Welcome to my renovation." I held the plastic sheet aside, so they could see the kitchen.

"I missed demolition," Austin wailed. "Presty! How could you betray me like this?"

"It was one of the perks of staying on guard duty," Preston said. "We have more work."

"You can do the honors, Austin." I pointed to the remaining cabinets.

"I guess that'll have to do," he huffed as he and Preston took the food into my dining room.

Concern flickered in Cal's eyes, and he wrapped his arms around me and kissed me. "This is really sudden. Are you okay?"

"Change is good." I brushed away the dust that I'd transferred to his shirt. "I've needed to remodel for a while."

Cal stepped back and gave me a look that clearly communicated our discussion about my mental state wasn't finished. "I questioned Holden Miller this afternoon. Bobbi Sue watched me like a hawk, but he swears he knows nothing about your wallpaper or who could've done it."

"Do you believe him?"

"Yes. He looked genuinely confused when I asked about the wallpaper and swore that he'd never do anything that destructive or work with anyone who would. I talked to Blake. His parents are wealthy, and he confirmed giving Holden the money."

"It's still hard to believe the pranks are a coincidence."

"Exactly. I canvassed our neighborhood to see if anyone noticed a car at your house this morning."

It seemed like a stretch to call the houses scattered throughout the area a neighborhood, but I supposed technically it was. "And?"

"No one who drove by saw anything unusual."

"Which doesn't tell us anything because I have barns and grain bins to park behind."

"I'm not finished," Cal said. "There's a couple more houses I'd like to hit this evening after we eat."

"May I come with you? Pretty please. If Arden is allowed to observe Vanessa, then shouldn't I be able to go with you?"

"Arden changed her mind," he said.

"Because of the background check?"

"She didn't give Vanessa a reason."

"She must be hiding something."

"Or she changed her mind."

I wasn't convinced the reason was that simple. "So may I tag along when you talk to my neighbors?"

"If you let me do the talking."

"Deal." I'd be spending a lot of time biting my tongue.

After supper, Cal and I drove a couple of miles west of my house in his work-issued car. He was whistling "Amazing Grace," and I always took comfort in hearing him.

Just like I had when my daddy had whistled.

"I'm assuming you know who lives on this farm?" Cal pointed to the pale green, two-story house, pole barn, and grain bin.

"You assume correctly—Jerry Fincher. Jerry never liked Daddy all that well—especially after Daddy beat him in a school board election."

Cal pulled into the driveway, and I spotted a for-sale sign in the yard and pointed. "I heard he's planning to retire, but I didn't realize he was selling his house."

We got out of the car. "Good evening, Mr. Fincher," Cal said.

Jerry sat in a wooden rocking chair on his front porch. Years of working in the sun had etched deep lines into his leathery face.

He had a large American flag tattooed on his forearm and wore a Richardville Aviation Club T-shirt.

"Evening." Jerry stood and surveyed me without even a hint of friendliness in his gaze. "You got a lot of nerve showing up on my property."

Was he mad about the election? That'd been fifteen years ago. I didn't see Jerry all that often except at the grain elevator now and then, so how could I have possibly offended him? "Sir?"

He pointed a finger at me. "Don't pretend to be all wide-eyed and innocent. You know what you did."

What'd I done? Then it hit me. Jerry used to farm the three hundred acres that Grandpa and I had begun cash renting from the Dillmans this past spring. "Is this about the Dillman farm?"

Jerry narrowed his eyes. "You stole it out from under me like your daddy stole that election years ago."

Beside me, Cal bristled.

"Joe Dillman asked me for a bid because he said you were retiring, so I gave him one." I didn't feel like dignifying the election comment with a response. Daddy had won by nearly five hundred votes, which was a landslide in our neck of the woods.

"I wasn't ready to retire. I was just thinking about it—and Joe knew that."

I crossed my arms. "It seems to me, your problem's with Joe —not me."

"I was plannin' to work for a few more years, but now I'm gonna have to retire and downsize, all because of you," he said. "Put my house on the market yesterday."

Could Jerry be the Wallpaper Bandit because he was heartbroken over being forced into retirement?

Clearing his throat, Cal removed his badge and introduced himself. "Sir, I'm investigating some mischief that took place in this neighborhood this morning. Mind if I ask a few questions about what you might've witnessed?"

"I do, but I'm not one to disrespect an officer of the law, so have at it."

Cal took out his phone and opened a note-taking app. "Did you happen to drive by Georgia's house this morning between eight-thirty and nine-thirty?"

"Nope. Since I had to retire, I was drinking my coffee right here on the porch."

"Did you witness anything out of the ordinary during that same time?" Cal asked.

Jerry squinted down the road, and a slow smirk replaced his annoyed expression. "I reckon I did. I saw a woman jogging, and she had legs for days that she was showing off in a pair of little blue shorts. Whoo boy!"

Cal's face remained expressionless, and I tried not to cringe. Could Diana Graham have been the runner? Was Arden a runner?

"Do you know who she was?" Cal asked.

"No. I've only been a free agent for about a year since my wife passed, but I've never seen a gal with legs like that running on this road before." He glanced at me, as if to communicate that my legs didn't meet his standards.

This didn't even come close to offending me, because I wouldn't be caught dead in a pair of running shorts.

Cal nodded. "Could you give me an approximate age?"

"Nope. She had on sunglasses, but I'd say she's a young thing with legs like that."

"What color was her hair?"

"Don't know. She was wearing a baseball cap."

Cal and I exchanged glances. "Do you remember what color the cap was? Or did you see a logo?" he asked.

"No idea."

That figured.

"Was her hair long or short?" Cal asked.

"Don't know. There might've been a ponytail. I was too focused on her legs. I'm a leg man."

That, ladies and gentlemen, went without saying. I literally had to bite my tongue to keep that snarky comment from flying free.

Nice Georgia.

"Do you want me to find out her name?" Jerry squared his shoulders. "She might jog by again, and I'd be happy to help."

I'll bet you would.

"Which way was she running?" Cal asked with a completely straight face.

How *ever* did he manage?

Jerry pointed east—toward my house.

"Did she happen to be carrying anything or wearing a backpack?" Cal asked.

"No—but hold on. She *was* pushing a jogging stroller, but I didn't get a good look at the kid because of the shade thingamajig."

He *had* been distracted if it'd taken him this long to recall that detail. It also meant if the jogger was the Wallpaper Bandit, she could've hidden the vinegar bottle and wallpaper scraps in the stroller.

Cal glanced at me. "Did she pass this way again?"

"If she did, I was inside and missed the show." Jerry stroked his chin. "Tell you what. Lorelei McPherson lives over there." He pointed to a bungalow across the road and to the west. "She's a real busybody, so I reckon she could tell you if there's anything odd going on."

"Thanks for your help, sir." Cal led me to his car and opened the door for me.

"That was awkward," I said as soon as we were both inside. "But Joe Dillman really did tell me Jerry was retiring, or I wouldn't have put in a bid for the land. That's not how Winstons operate."

"I know."

"It crossed my mind that Jerry could be the Wallpaper Bandit if he were heartbroken over having to retire, but that's probably a stretch."

Cal headed toward Lorelei's house. "Has Jerry ever been inside your house?"

"He could've been when my parents lived there, but I doubt it since he didn't like Daddy. Plus, Jerry has no way of knowing that I haven't updated my kitchen." I glanced out at the soybean field. "I'm not convinced Jerry's all that devastated about retirement. Seems like he just wanted to give me a piece of his mind."

"I thought the same thing."

"Do you think he's telling the truth about the jogger?"

"I don't know," Cal said. "His statement about the stroller seemed tacked on. Is he the kind to make up stories?"

"Perhaps—if he wanted to send you on a wild goose chase to get back at me."

Cal parked in Lorelei McPherson's driveway. She lived in a brick ranch with a small porch, and her front door displayed an elaborate pink and yellow floral wreath.

After Cal rang the bell, the door cracked open, and a pudgy woman with frizzy blond hair puffing around her face stuck her head out.

"Are you Lorelei McPherson?" Cal asked.

"Who wants to know?"

Cal flashed his badge.

"I didn't do anything wrong. Go away." She slammed the door.

"You've got to be kidding me," I muttered.

Cal knocked. "Ma'am, I need to ask you some questions about

an incident that took place in the neighborhood this morning. You're a potential witness. Please open up."

The door cracked again. "That's all?" She looked back and forth between us. "This ain't about the speeding ticket I got yesterday?"

"I wasn't even aware of that, ma'am. We don't have to come in. You can talk to us right here."

She lifted her chin. "I slowed down as soon as I saw the speed limit sign, and it's not my fault there's a tree branch blocking it. Do you think the county would trim that tree? No—all because some Barney Fife wants to make his quota. I told him I'd be going to court to fight the ticket, and he didn't take too kindly to that."

"And you thought he sent someone to stop you?" I asked.

"You can't be too careful nowadays." She swung the door open. "Come on in. No sense in air conditioning the outside."

Cal introduced us as we stepped into a tiny living room where an episode of *Three's Company* was playing on the TV and a worn leather sectional lined two walls. A parakeet swooped in from the hall and landed on Lorelei's shoulder. She barely seemed to notice.

"I'm sorry for your frustration over the speeding ticket, ma'am," Cal said. "Are you familiar with the Winston farm down the road?"

"Pass it all the time on my way to Wildcat Springs."

"Did you drive by this morning between eight-thirty and nine-thirty?" he asked.

"Nope. I left for work in Richardville around twenty to nine, so I went to the west."

"Did you pass a woman running with a jogging stroller?"

"Absolutely," Lorelei said. "She was coming east, and I slowed down, because I don't like it when cars go zooming by me when I'm out for a walk. I wanted to be extra careful because of the stroller."

"Did you recognize her?" Cal asked.

"Can't say as I did. I'd never seen her running out here before. She had on a baseball cap and sunglasses, but I thought, *I wish I was that skinny.*" Lorelei shook her head. "I did notice one weird thing, though. As hot as it was, she had a blanket draped over her kid's stroller."

CHAPTER ELEVEN

A blanket-covered jogging stroller would be a perfect hiding place for shredded wallpaper and a bottle of vinegar.

Or the jogger could've been a mother protecting her baby from the sun.

"Do you remember anything else about her?" Cal asked.

"No," Lorelei said. "Did she do something wrong?"

"Not necessarily, but she may be a witness to a crime." He handed her a card. "Call if you think of anything else." He opened the front door.

"What crime?" Lorelei asked.

"Someone broke into my house and vandalized my kitchen," I said.

Lorelei gaped at me. "Why would someone do that?"

"That's what we're trying to figure out." Cal stepped outside onto the porch.

"I'll keep my ears open," she said.

We returned to his car as the setting sun painted the sky with orange and purple streaks.

"Arden and Diana are both thin, and Arden was wearing a

baseball cap on Sunday night. However, Diana has legs that she likes to show off, and I overheard her say she'd been jogging this morning," I said as Cal drove toward my house. "What do you think?"

"We need to figure out who the jogger is—as soon as possible."

The next morning after breakfast, Preston left for the office, but Austin took his laptop and coffee mug to my back porch to work.

After I called for a dumpster, I hurried outside, staked Gus next to my garden, and picked green beans before the sunny day grew hotter. I'd just filled a second grocery bag when I heard gravel pop under tires. A door slammed, and a grim-faced Hamlet crossed my yard.

Austin stood, folded his arms, and stared menacingly at Hamlet.

Uh-oh. I set the bags aside, untethered Gus, and jogged toward my house with the dog leading the way.

"Say the word, and he's out of here," Austin muttered.

"Easy there, killer. Let's see what he wants before you put him flat on his back." I brushed dirt from the knees of my jeans and straightened my hat while Gus greeted Hamlet by jumping on him.

"Hello, Georgia Rae. Austin. I'm glad you're here." Hamlet held onto the dog's front paws and gazed at me with concern. "I had a visit from your boyfriend this morning regarding your kitchen vandalism."

"You've got to be kidding me." I closed my eyes. Hadn't Cal told me he *didn't* suspect Hamlet? What'd changed? Last I knew, Cal was going to try to figure out who the mystery jogger was. "I'm sorry. I never dreamed Cal would accuse you—"

"There were no accusations." Hamlet let go of Gus. "Cal wants to figure out what's happening to you, and he's right to question me after learning about my brother leaving the beef heart on your porch."

"Because Holden and his buddy might've lied to cover for you?"

"That was my impression. That's *not* what happened, but a good detective needs to rule out that possibility," Hamlet said. "I suspect Cal was concerned that I might've heard about Holden's prank and decided to take the torture a step further by vandalizing your kitchen."

Austin relaxed his tense posture, but his eyes remained alert.

I clenched my fists. "But you wouldn't do that. Look at Gus sitting there next to you. He wouldn't be glad to see you if he knew you'd broken into my house."

"Exonerated by the guard dog." Hamlet patted Gus's head.

"I can't believe Cal questioned you." I huffed. "He told me you weren't a suspect." Was Cal worried I still had feelings for Hamlet? Was he trying to get back at Hamlet for dating me? Cal had given us his blessing, for heaven's sake.

"It's fine," Hamlet said.

"You're not mad?"

"Not at all."

"You look mad." I studied his expression. "Or at least peeved." Hamlet could be pretty inscrutable.

"I'm furious that someone's messing with you," Hamlet said.

"I appreciate that." Then I remembered what I'd been wanting to ask Hamlet. "Is there a reason Diana Graham isn't your biggest fan?"

His eyes clouded. "She believes I've stolen business from her and was put out when Cal chose me to renovate his kitchen instead of hiring her team."

Cal had never said anything to me about that, but he might not have known Diana had been upset.

"I heard that she's tried to ruin my reputation by spreading lies about my work." Hamlet shook his head. "Diana even convinced Arden to cancel our dinner date. I met Arden at Pastry Delight and had no idea they were sisters until that happened."

That must've been what Holden had been reluctant to tell the twins and me, and it explained Arden's reaction to Hamlet at Bible study. But what in the world did Hamlet see in Arden, of all women? "You can do better than Arden."

"I certainly wasn't impressed with her behavior at your house. Speaking of which, I apologize for not asking if I could bring Wolfe. I thought he could use some new friends since he moved here from Florida."

"No worries. Maybe he and Arden will get together."

"Opposites certainly do attract."

Then, Hamlet's comment sank in. Wolfe was from Florida. Chuck Richman's cousin Travis had lived in Florida. Could Wolfe be Travis seeking revenge for his cousin's death? "One more question," I said. "Is Wolfe Sommers a stage name?"

"I've never asked. Why?"

I shrugged, trying my hardest to appear nonchalant. "Just wondering, because it sounds like it could be."

"You may be right." He shifted. "So, Brandi told me you tore your kitchen apart yesterday, and I see the evidence." He motioned toward the trash pile behind my garage.

I ducked my head. "That was sort of impulsive, and Preston was here to help."

"I missed out on the fun." Austin's scowl deepened.

"Let me handle the renovation," Hamlet said. "I have some time before I have to be in Chicago to film the movie, and I'll charge a reasonable price. Quite frankly, I could use the money for my move."

I met his kind, blue-gray eyes. "Are you sure?"

"Certainly. We're still friends, and you'll always hold a special place in my heart."

That was sweet of him. "I do like the work you did on Cal's kitchen, and Ashley could help with the design."

"Good. I'll be in touch." He turned toward his truck and fished his keys from his pocket.

"Wait. Take some green beans." I swiped up a bag and handed it to him.

"Thanks. Take care, Georgia Rae." He strolled to his truck.

"Are you sure you want him to renovate your kitchen when Cal sees him as a suspect?" Austin asked as Hamlet drove away.

I picked up the remaining bag of green beans and carried it into my garage, while Austin and Gus followed. I opened the refrigerator door. "Hamlet wouldn't hurt me and can take a shift as my bodyguard if we don't catch the Wallpaper Bandit by then." I set the beans inside. "Cal will have to get over it."

"Whatever you say, sissy." He looked at his phone. "I have to go to the office this afternoon, and Preston's with clients. Do you want to tag along?"

I was impressed he took his guard duty so seriously. "I can't. Grandpa's coming over, and we're going to scout crops with my drone. I'll take Gus with us, and it should take most of the afternoon." I'd have to drive my vehicle because Grandpa wouldn't want Gus spreading hair on his seats and leaving his nose-print graffiti all over the windows.

"Good." Austin stroked the dog's head. "Because I don't think he should be alone either."

⸻

That afternoon when Gus, Grandpa, and I arrived at home, Austin's Jeep was parked in the driveway, so I told Grandpa he didn't need to come in and check for the boogeyman. As I stepped inside, the smell of garlic and tomato lingered in the air. Austin must've heated leftovers from last night using the microwave that we'd moved to the dining room.

But for no particular reason, a chill traveled my spine. Something felt—off.

I wound Gus's leash tighter around my hand and patted my back pocket to check for my phone.

"Austin?"

The silence thickened.

I shoved the plastic aside and stepped into my living room. No note on the table—or chalk wall in my dining room. My phone didn't have any missed text messages.

With Gus leading the way, I pounded upstairs.

"Austin?"

I opened the guest room door. Clothes were strewn on the floor and spilled out of his gigantic suitcase. A dress shirt hung on the closet door handle. Gus lunged for a wadded sock, but I yanked him back.

The door to the Jack-and-Jill bath was closed, so I rapped on it. "Austin? Are you okay?"

Silence.

"Austin? Seriously. I'm about three seconds from coming in, so you'd better answer. This isn't funny."

One.

Two.

Three.

I opened the door and screeched.

Austin lay sprawled on the floor next to the toilet.

CHAPTER TWELVE

He lifted his head and stared at me with glassy eyes. Sweat beaded on his face, and he clutched his stomach.

"What happened?" I knelt beside him while Gus sniffed.

"Wanted a snack. Ate casserole about an hour ago. Started feeling terrible." With the back of his hand, he wiped leaking saliva from his mouth and groaned. "Stomach hurts." He shoved Gus away.

"What casserole? You mean leftovers from Salvador's?"

"Those were gone. Casserole from Brandi."

I froze. Brandi hadn't said anything about making a casserole. A wave of dizziness passed through my vision, and I tried to focus on my phone. Brandi had brought me plenty of food through the years, and she'd even dropped it off a time or two when I wasn't home. But I was sure after everything that'd happened, she wouldn't do that now. Not to mention, she'd begun her new job today and didn't have time.

And how would she have gotten into my garage to leave the food?

With my heart thumping, I dialed 9-1-1 and pressed my shaky fingers against Austin's neck to check his pulse.

Weak.

Please, God. Help him.

"Nine-one-one. What's your emergency?"

"This is Georgia Winston. My stepbrother may've been poisoned from something he ate about an hour ago."

Austin moaned.

"He's conscious. Sweating profusely and complaining of abdominal pain. His pulse is weak, and his skin looks a little blue. He's twenty-five and in good health as far as I know. Please. Just send an ambulance." I gave my address and disconnected before the dispatcher could tell me to stay on the line. I wet a washcloth with cold water and wiped his face.

"What's happening?" Austin asked.

"An ambulance is coming. If I help, can you make it downstairs?"

He curled into a tighter ball.

I rewet the washcloth and stooped beside him. "I'm sorry I live in the middle of nowhere. Hang on."

"Trying. Don't want to die." He closed his eyes.

I clasped his hand. "Lord, help the ambulance get here quickly. Please help the doctors heal Austin."

"Amen," he mumbled.

"What kind of casserole was it?" I dabbed the cloth over his neck.

"Don't know." He didn't open his eyes.

"What was in it?"

"Pasta. Other stuff. Don't remember."

I tapped Cal's number, and thankfully he answered. "I need you at my house," I said before he could even say hello. "Austin's been poisoned with a casserole he thought came from Brandi, and I've called an ambulance."

"I'm coming right now." He disconnected.

In the distance, I heard sirens but stayed with Austin until the sound grew closer. "I'll be right back. I don't want the ambulance to miss the house."

He groaned.

With Gus on my heels, I ran downstairs. I tossed a biscuit in his crate and slammed the door behind him. Then, I sprinted outside into my yard and waved the ambulance into the driveway.

———

As the ambulance was leaving my driveway, Cal arrived. He hopped out of his car and gathered me in his arms.

I rested my head on his shoulder and didn't want to move from his embrace. But we had a case to solve, so I stepped back. "Austin thought Brandi put the casserole in my fridge, but it couldn't have come from her because we changed the locks and security code, and she doesn't have a new key or code. She wouldn't break in through my garage door, which is the only other way someone could've gotten in without tripping the alarm."

"I know." He removed an evidence bag from his car and donned a pair of gloves as we entered the garage. "I'm mad at myself for not thinking about securing your garage door. It's not that hard for someone to use a coat hanger or a piece of wire to trip the emergency latch."

"How is this person always one step ahead of us?" I wailed. "I thought we were smart changing the locks and getting a video doorbell, but neither one did a bit of good." I held up my phone. "How is the doorbell camera showing nothing?"

"Whoever did this probably used a wireless jammer that stopped the camera from recording."

"Well that's just great."

"We'll figure it out." Cal approached my refrigerator.

A flower bordered note—with Brandi's initials—was stuck to the door. Without touching, I examined the paper.

Thought you could use some food for your guests. Casserole in fridge.

> *Love,*
> *Brandi*

"Is this her handwriting?" he asked.

"It's similar but doesn't look quite right since it's printed." I took a picture. "I've seen those custom sticky notes in her kitchen, but most of the time, she writes in cursive if she's leaving a note."

Cal yanked open the refrigerator, and when I peered inside, my stomach plummeted. A disposable foil container rested next to the green beans.

Through the plastic lid, I spotted rigatoni noodles in a tomato-based meat sauce with green peppers and mushrooms. "That looks like one of Brandi's recipes. The last time Preston and Austin stayed with me, Brandi brought food, and she made cookies for me yesterday, so I can see why Austin fell for the note." I gasped. "Maybe that's the whole point."

"What?"

"What if whoever left this casserole never intended it for me but meant to fool the *twins*? Brandi hates mushrooms, and I know she *never* uses them in her cooking, but Austin and Preston don't."

"It's also possible this person used mushrooms because some kinds are poisonous." Cal removed the foil container and slipped it into an evidence bag. "I've seen that before. I'll get a sample to the hospital, so they know how to treat Austin."

"I never should've let the guys stay here." I clutched my

braid. "Why'd I think it was a good idea to renovate? It's my fault the refrigerator is in the garage. If I'd left everything alone, then the person couldn't have put the casserole in the fridge. I covered my face with my hands. "Austin can't die. He just can't."

Cal put his arm around me as he led me out of the garage. "I haven't stopped praying for him since you called me."

Then another thought hit me, and I lifted my head. "I haven't called Preston or Dan and Mom and Makayla. And I should let my Bible study group know, so they can pray. And I need to get to the hospital, but I don't want to leave Gus alone."

"Sweetheart, one step at a time. I'll get someone out here to look for more evidence, and I'll drive to the hospital while you make calls. Why don't you see if J.T. will watch Gus? We can drop him off on the way."

I nodded, my throat too swollen to speak.

Mom and Dan raced into Richard County Hospital's emergency room and made a beeline to the corner that I'd staked out, away from the other folks in the waiting room. Cal had given the doctor a sample of the casserole before he left for the sheriff's department.

"Has there been any word yet?" Dan asked.

"No," I said.

Dan and Mom exchanged glances before he walked away and found a nurse.

"I don't understand how Austin might've eaten poisonous mushrooms in a casserole at your house." Mom sat beside me. "Did you try to cook with them and accidently use the wrong kind?"

Seriously? I wasn't *that* inept in the kitchen. "No."

"Are you chasing another mystery?"

"Not on purpose. I'll explain when Dan gets back." I rested my elbows on my knees and waited in silence until Dan joined us.

"The nurse told me that the doctor on duty has been practicing for thirty years and has seen some cases of mushroom poisoning in his day," Dan's voice trembled, and tears sprang into his eyes. "He thinks that since Austin got quick medical attention, he'll recover."

Mom squeezed his hand. "Thank God."

Yes, thank you Lord. "Did she say anything else?" I asked.

"The rapid onset of symptoms point to some type of inocybe mushroom, but that's all we know so far." He cleared his throat. "I just can't understand how this happened. What's going on, Georgia?"

I fought against a guilt tsunami. "There have been a couple of incidents the last few days." I explained about the beef heart, the stripped wallpaper, and how I'd changed my locks and security codes and added a video doorbell. "Even with the precautions, Preston and Austin offered to stay and protect me. Because they were there, I had them help me demo the kitchen for a renovation. We moved the fridge to the garage, and I never dreamed someone would break open my garage door and plant a poisoned casserole with a fake note from Brandi."

Mom and Dan were silent. I wished they'd say something. Anything.

"Cal's investigating."

"Why didn't you tell us?" Dan asked.

"What could you have done?"

"Upgraded your security system, for one," he said.

"Like I said, I already added a video doorbell and changed the locks and security code, so clearly, that's not a deterrent to whoever's behind this." I pressed my hand to my mouth.

"And you have no idea why this is happening?" Mom asked.

I twisted my amethyst ring. "It may have to do with the fact that I got back together with Cal, but we don't really know."

Dan and Mom looked at each other, and she crossed her arms. "What happened to Hamlet?" she asked.

"He wants to chase an acting career. I want to stay in Wildcat Springs."

"How long ago did this happen?"

I picked a hangnail and mumbled, "A few weeks ago."

"He was awfully good to you. You never considered following him?" Mom fiddled with her leather and pearl bracelet. "You could always be a music teacher. Your dad and I paid good money for that college education you've never used."

Why was she bringing that up now? "Obviously, I considered all of those things, just like Hamlet thought about staying in Wildcat Springs for me. But we weren't in love, and God is leading us in different directions."

"Love is a choice," she said. "You could've learned to love Hamlet."

"I could've, but we decided *together* that we're better as friends."

"After the way Cal treated you, I can't understand why you'd take him back," she said. "Is it because you're lonely?"

"No, I lov—"

"He's not the only eligible bachelor around. You could try online dating again."

Right. Because that'd been such a smashing success when I'd tried it before.

"Do you really want to be with a man whose profession could put your life in danger?" she demanded.

Dan rested a hand on Mom's arm. "Jill, this isn't—"

"Don't." She shoved his hand away. "Your son is fighting for his life because my daughter insists on sticking her nose where it doesn't belong and getting back together with a man who couldn't commit to her the first time around."

My blood pressure skyrocketed. "That's *not* what's happening right now." With my pulse whacking my neck, I shot out of my chair and stomped toward the vending machines before I said something I regretted—or dropped dead from a stroke.

I tried to focus my scattering thoughts. The rational part of me understood that an evil person was behind this chaos, and that I wasn't responsible, no matter who I'd chosen to date.

But what if I was telling myself that to feel better? Was Mom right, and I was to blame for this situation? I considered the poem's words. *A mystery for Georgia Rae. Who'll jump right into the fray.* Someone knew my history of crime solving. Was that why I was a target?

For the millionth time in the last decade, I wished Daddy were here to advise me because he'd always understood me.

Help me, Lord. Heal Austin.

In spite of my trembling fingers, I unearthed some change from my purse and bought M&Ms from the vending machine. I ripped open the package and downed a palmful.

Prayer and chocolate were my favorite therapy.

I dropped into a chair far from my mom and Dan and checked my text messages. J.T. had sent a picture of Gus sprawled on the couch with his paws in the air. At least I didn't need to worry about my dog.

The emergency room doors slid open, and Preston raced toward Mom and Dan. I got up and moved closer.

As I approached, Preston's stricken expression broke my heart. "What do we know?" His eyes darted wildly.

Dan told them what he'd learned from the nurse.

Preston mashed his fist into his palm. "This is so messed up. It's like this sicko wants you to know none of your friends or family are safe either."

My friends. Brandi.

What kind of friend was I? I hadn't called her yet, and she needed to know what was happening.

"What's wrong, Georgia?" Dan asked.

"Whoever did this might've been in Brandi's house," I said. "There was a sticky note on my refrigerator like the ones in her kitchen."

Preston stilled. "Have you told her?"

"No." I clutched my phone. "I was going to call her on the way to the hospital, but by the time I talked to all of you, we were here, and I was so distracted about Austin that I didn't put the pieces together like I should've." How had I ever managed to help solve any cases?

I tapped her number, and after she didn't pick up, I tried calling the school. However, no one answered, so I dialed her cell again and left a message telling her to call me back as soon as possible and not to go home without talking to me first. Then, Preston and I sat in silence with our parents, staring at the talking head on a cable news station.

The nurse approached us a while later. "Mr. and Mrs. Farthing? The doctors have stabilized your son if you'd like to see him. We're going to admit him when we get a room assignment. The rest of you will need to wait to see him, though." She looked between Preston and me.

"You and Preston go first," Mom said to Dan, then turned to the nurse. "I'm just the stepmom, and he's very close to his twin."

"Of course." The nurse offered an understanding smile.

As the nurse led Dan and Preston away, Cal returned, and I hurried over to him before he could get any closer to my mom. "Austin's stable," I blurted. "We need to check on Brandi. I tried calling her, but she hasn't answered. Someone had to have gotten into her house, and—"

"I'm going there next." He wrapped his arms around me. "Do you want to come? She'll want to see that you're okay."

"Yes. I need to tell my mom." I lowered my voice. "She found out we're dating again, and she's not happy. She's just scared over everything that's happened and will come around—eventually." At least, I hoped so.

"I see." He rested his hand on my back. "Let me say hello—avoiding her won't help." We approached my mom, and her face remained expressionless.

"Detective."

"Mrs. Farthing, I'm doing everything in my power to find the person responsible for poisoning Austin."

"I'm certain you are. I've never doubted your competence. How could I? You helped put away my husband's murderer."

I knew better than to be encouraged because I sensed a *but* on the horizon.

"But that doesn't mean I'm thrilled that my daughter's in a relationship with you again." She stood. "Excuse me."

"Mom, wait."

"Yes?"

"We're going to check on Brandi."

"Fine. One of us will keep you posted." She stalked toward the restroom.

Cal and I plodded outside in silence, where the humidity smacked us in the face.

"The E.R. doctor thought Austin's symptoms were consistent with poisoning from some type of inocybe mushroom, and with medical treatment, his prognosis is good," I said as we got into the car.

"Good."

"So . . . whoever put the mushrooms in the casserole either knew that it was possible to survive the poisoning and didn't intend to kill him or just botched the job. But I'm not convinced the person responsible is stupid enough to make a mistake like that."

"I tend to agree." Cal drove onto the highway. "Poisoning the casserole with mushrooms could be the perpetrator's way of letting you know that you're not safe—even with the Twin Menaces guarding you. There are plenty of highly effective poisons that aren't that hard to obtain that could've easily killed Austin right away." He glanced at me. "I'm sorry. That was blunt."

"But true." I squeezed my hands together and shuddered at the thought of Austin eating the pasta, which he loved. "Hold on."

"What?"

"Wolfe Sommers. Remember he said, 'I love me some pasta,' and wanted the chicken spaghetti recipe on Sunday?"

"Because of *that,* you think he made the poisoned casserole?"

"Maybe," I said. "We at least know he can cook."

"But why would he want to hurt you by getting to your step-brothers?"

"What if Wolfe is a stage name, and he's Chuck Richman's cousin Travis? Maybe he killed Natalie and is ready to get rid of me."

"Not likely."

"But Hamlet told me he doesn't know if Wolfe's a stage name, and he's from Florida—like Travis." Even as I said the words, I realized they were a stretch.

Cal glanced in the rearview mirror and changed lanes. "When did you talk to Hamlet?"

"He stopped by my house this morning. I certainly hope the casserole incident means you can rule him out a suspect."

"Didn't waste any time, did he?"

I scowled. "He was just checking on me and apologizing for

bringing Wolfe to Bible study without asking. He even offered to renovate my kitchen."

"I suppose you took him up on it."

"Yes. Why shouldn't I? He did a good job on yours. Are you not happy with the work he did on your kitchen?"

"He did a fine job."

"Then what's your problem?"

"He doesn't have an alibi for the time your kitchen was vandalized."

"Oh, for heaven's sake." I rolled my eyes. "Even if by some stretch of the imagination, Hamlet was inspired by his brother leaving the beef heart on my porch and decided to sneak into my house to strip the wallpaper and write a limerick on the wall, you actually think he would've put a poisoned casserole in my refrigerator with the hope of hurting my stepbrothers?"

"It doesn't matter what I think," Cal said. "It matters what the evidence says."

"There's a lot more evidence for Hamlet being a wonderful Christian man than there is for his being the crazy psycho who's behind all of this! Besides, he's moved on. He told me he asked Arden out on a date, even though she cancelled after Diana made her."

"Why would Diana do that?" He zoomed through a yellow light.

"She didn't like it when Hamlet got the job renovating your kitchen instead of her." I huffed. "You never told me that."

"We weren't dating at the time, and it never occurred to me that I should. I already told you I avoid Diana at all costs. In fact, I asked Vanessa to find out where Diana was jogging yesterday morning—and she was at the gym during the time your wallpaper was stripped."

That was fantastic. "So you moved on to Hamlet. Have you already checked to see if he has an alibi for this afternoon?"

"I absolutely will."

I crossed my arms, stared out the window at McDonald's, and prayed Hamlet had an alibi. Not because I doubted his innocence but because I wanted Cal to move on from the Hamlet-as-a jilted-lover theory. "Have you even looked into Arden's background?"

"Yes."

"And?"

His jaw ticked—again. "She's exactly who she says she is, and there's zero evidence she ever lived in the Cleveland area or knew Chuck Richman."

"That doesn't mean she isn't out to get me, so I don't think we should rule her out."

"We?"

"Excuse me." I gritted my teeth. "You and Vanessa shouldn't rule her out. After all, she brought you cinnamon rolls, so she must know how to cook."

"I told my mom about what's happening, and she'll be here tomorrow," he said.

Nice subject change. "Oh, good." I gave myself a mental pat on the back for not sounding nearly as sarcastic as I felt.

"You sure about that?" He stopped at a red light and surveyed me.

"Yep." I met his gaze.

His look clearly communicated he wasn't buying what I was trying to sell.

But right now, I didn't give a rat's rump if he believed me or not.

CHAPTER THIRTEEN

When Cal and I arrived at Brandi's brick, split-level home in Sycamore Hills, Cal's partner Vanessa Hawk-Remington climbed out of her car.

We greeted the willowy and auburn-haired Vanessa, who, as usual, looked more like she should be a runway model than a detective. When she'd first worked with Cal, I'd been glad to learn that she was engaged. Now she was a happy newlywed.

Vanessa hustled up the sidewalk and knocked on the door. Brandi, holding her Yorkie Gigi, answered, and her forehead creased with confusion as she surveyed us. Obviously, she hadn't gotten my message, but I was thankful she appeared to be fine.

"May we come in and ask you a few questions, Mrs. Hartfield?" Vanessa asked.

"Of course." She stepped aside and motioned toward the couch. "What's going on?" she mouthed to me behind Cal and Vanessa's backs.

"Psycho struck again," I mouthed.

Her eyes widened, and she freed Gigi. The dog ran straight to me, and I bent and scratched her behind the ears.

"Mrs. Hartfield, did you make a casserole and take it to Georgia's home earlier today?" Vanessa perched on the couch.

I bristled at the question. Did she really suspect Brandi?

"No." Brandi looked at me with surprise. "I didn't have time. I just became the high school principal and was at school all day for a technology conference."

"What time did you arrive at the school?" Vanessa asked.

Brandi squinted. "After I bought muffin and Danish trays at Pastry Delight, I got to the school around seven-thirty this morning. The sessions finished at four, but I stayed until five helping to clean up."

"Can you give me some names of people who saw you?" Vanessa asked.

Brandi listed the names of several teachers and the assistant principal. "Do you mind telling me what this is about?"

"Someone put a poisoned rigatoni casserole in Georgia's refrigerator and left a note written on your stationery with your signature," Cal said.

I showed her the picture of the note.

Brandi gasped. "But I didn't write that—or make a casserole. I haven't even had time to go grocery shopping for myself since I got back from Europe." She looked at me. "Wait . . . How do you know it was poisoned?"

"Austin ate some," I said.

Brandi's hand flew to her mouth. "Is he . . .?"

"He's at the hospital in stable condition and is expected to recover," Cal said.

Tears flooded her eyes as she faced Cal. "You know I didn't do this, right? I would never hurt anyone. What type of poison?" She swiped under her eyes.

"Possibly muscarine—from mushrooms," Vanessa said. "We're waiting for confirmation, however."

"I hate mushrooms and don't cook with them." Brandi's voice held a note of panic.

"Georgia mentioned that to Cal," Vanessa said. "Please relax, ma'am. We're just trying to be thorough. Who has keys to your house?"

"Georgia, Ashley, my parents, and my sister Carly."

"No one else . . . like a cleaning lady?" Vanessa asked.

"No." Brandi scooped up the dog. "I do all my cleaning myself. It's therapeutic."

"Do you have a security system that I'm not seeing?" Vanessa glanced around.

"No. But I have my gun and a permit to carry." She stroked Gigi's head. "And guard dog, here."

Vanessa turned to me. "Where do you keep Brandi's key?"

"On the rack by my back door—and it's labeled." My stomach tightened. "Whoever entered my house to strip the wallpaper could've taken it."

"Or someone Brandi invited into her home stole a sticky note," Cal said. "Where do you keep the notepad?"

"I'll show you." She motioned for us to follow her into the kitchen, where she pointed at a built-in desk next to her back door. "Right there."

"Have you hosted your Bible study group or any other people recently?" Cal asked.

Why didn't he come right out and ask her if Hamlet had been here? It was completely obvious that was what he was thinking.

"Not since May. I was in Europe for six weeks this summer."

"The other night at Bible study, you mentioned Arden Tanner is your neighbor," Cal said. "Has she been in your house recently?"

Brandi's eyes widened. "She was here last night because one of the characters in her mystery novel is a historian, and since she knew I taught history, she asked if I had a book on the Revolutionary War she could borrow for research. I do and told her she could use it."

"Did you leave her alone to go get it?" Vanessa asked.

"Yes. The book was in my basement office," Brandi said. "But how would Arden—or someone else—fake my handwriting?"

"It's possible someone used things you'd already written as a model." Vanessa looked around the kitchen, before crossing over to the refrigerator and removing a magnetic notepad from the door. "Do you always keep a running grocery list?" She held out the list for us to see.

Brandi had printed *bread, garlic, flour, tomatoes, honey, fruit,* and *milk.*

"Yes."

I studied the list, comparing it to the words in the note. "If Arden is our culprit, all she needed to do was take a picture of the list, and she had nearly all the letters of the alphabet in Brandi's handwriting."

Brandi closed her eyes. "I know Arden's odd, but I didn't know she might be dangerous, or I never would've let her in. I should've known it was weird that she'd ask me for a book instead of going to the library."

"We don't know she's guilty, because someone could've used Georgia's copy of your key to get one of your sticky notes," Vanessa said. "For all we know, Arden was using the book as an excuse to make a friend."

"I suppose." Brandi didn't sound convinced.

"Brandi, you and Gigi had better find another place to stay until you have a chance to change your locks," Cal said.

"I can go to my parents' house," Brandi whispered. "Will you wait while I pack a bag?"

"I'd be happy to," he said.

"We need to tell Ashley," I said. "I have a key to her house, and it may've been compromised too."

"Does she have a security system?" Cal asked.

"No," Brandi and I said in unison.

Brandi freed her dog and motioned for me to follow her up the short staircase. As soon as we were in her bedroom, she shut the door. "I can't believe a creepy stranger may have been in my house—and in yours."

I plunked onto her bed. "I'm sorry. This is all my fault."

She opened her closet and removed a duffel bag from a shelf. "How? You didn't ask to be targeted."

"At some point during my nosing around, I've made somebody mad. At least, that's my mom's conclusion, and considering the limerick, I'm not sure she's wrong." I told Brandi about the conversation in the emergency room.

"Your mom's just scared and stressed. If it helps, I believe you and Cal make a great match."

"You might not think that if you'd heard us fighting on the way here. Cal suspects Hamlet."

The color drained from Brandi's face. "Cal truly suspects him, or he questioned him because he's being thorough?"

I studied her. "You don't think that's completely ridiculous?"

"Of course I do," she said quickly. "But because of his job, Cal has to approach this situation differently than you and I would."

"I know." But it didn't make me feel any better.

She removed a couple of T-shirts from their hangers. "Isn't it just as likely somebody from Cal's past is targeting you to get to him? Didn't you tell us that happened with his friend Mason?"

"Yes. We've been hoping that wasn't the case, and Cal's looking into that possibility. His mom's coming tomorrow to help. Yay." I pumped my fist with fake enthusiasm.

"Her experience will be valuable." She opened a drawer and tossed some underwear and pajamas into the bag. "And she likes you."

"I know," I said. "Yvonne's the least of my worries. I feel terrible this is affecting Austin—and you and Ashley."

"We'll have to pray that God will fix this. He's trustworthy, and none of this has taken him by surprise." She took a dress from her closet and stuck it in a garment bag.

Even though I knew she was right, I was having trouble believing it. "Why is this happening when Cal and I just got back together? I don't know why I ever hoped things could end right for me or that I could be happy."

Brandi dropped a pair of sandals into the bag and faced me. "I'm going to ask you a question that I doubt you'll like, but I'm going to do it anyway."

Uh-oh. That was never good. "Go ahead."

"Where's your hope?"

"My hope? Like I'm acting hopeless? If you had your kitchen vandalized and your stepbrother was poisoned and it might all have to do with your new relationship, wouldn't you feel like your chance at happiness had passed you by?"

She stared at me.

"Oh."

Brandi *did* have an equivalent to my trauma. No, equivalent wasn't the right word because hers was much worse. She hadn't married until her thirties. Then, a few years into her marriage, her husband was killed in a car accident. Even now, she struggled to find a good man while Ashley and I were seeing our love lives fall into place. This was her gentle way of reminding me that while the new developments with Cal were wonderful, there was only One in whom I could truly place my hope.

Anything else was futile.

I'd been so wrapped up in Cal that I'd been doing a pretty lousy job of that lately.

"When you get a chance, read Psalm thirty-one," she said.

"Okay. And could you pray for me?"

She smiled gently. "Always."

When Brandi finished packing, we rejoined Cal and Vanessa in the living room.

"While you were upstairs, I called the guys who are going over Georgia's house for evidence," Cal said as we walked out the front door. "Your key and Ashley's key are still hanging on the rack by the door to the garage. However, someone could've used an app to copy the keys without taking them."

"Then I guess it's good I'm leaving." Brandi scooped up her dog and locked the door.

She wanted to go with us to check on Ashley before going on to her parents' house, and since I was still annoyed with Cal, I rode with Brandi on the short drive to Ashley's bungalow near downtown Wildcat Springs.

When we arrived, Ashley's expression grew concerned as she let us into her living room that was decorated with her own artwork and black lacquer and mother-of-pearl furniture pieces her mother had brought from South Korea. She wore flannel pajama shorts and a University of Kentucky T-shirt. "Is Austin worse?"

Clearly, she'd talked to J.T.

"No." Cal explained what we'd figured out and how her home might be compromised as well. "Have you noticed anything missing or out of place?"

"No. I haven't." She picked up her orange tabby Norman.

"Come stay with my parents and me," Brandi said. "I already asked, and they'd be happy to host you and Norman."

Ashley looked at Cal. "Is that what you think is best?"

"Yes. Whoever this person is, their behavior is escalating, and we've already seen a willingness to use one of Georgia's friends to try to get to her."

Brandi shuddered. "It's so creepy. It's like whoever is doing this has studied Georgia and her friends, so they know what we might do before we even do it."

"Exactly," Cal said.

A chill traveled over my entire body. It was more than studying. It was inside knowledge.

"What's wrong, hon? You're super pale," Ashley said.

As Cal put his arm around me, I tried to collect my scattered thoughts. "We've suspected Wolfe because he was in my kitchen, knew it was outdated, and could've overheard Holden and Blake talking about the beef heart prank. The same is true for Arden. I talked to Diana Graham at the hardware store about renovating my kitchen. I even used the words 'time for a change,' and the limerick used that phrase, but Diana was at the gym when my kitchen was vandalized."

"Yes," Cal said.

"But I also said the same thing about my kitchen on Sunday when Preston asked me if I was ever going to update, which was why I thought he and Austin might've pranked me."

Cal nodded as if he were somehow following my jumbled reasoning.

I squeezed the bridge of my nose. "Then, this person had to know Brandi is the type to bring food to her friends, that she'd be at work all day today, that I'd moved my refrigerator to the garage because of the renovation, and that the twins and I wouldn't be at my house this afternoon. If the twins were the intended target, then the psycho needed to be certain I wouldn't be there to stop

Austin from eating a casserole that I would've immediately found suspicious." I paused, and when they didn't answer, I rushed ahead. "Not a single person we've considered as a suspect—or anyone else—could've *possibly* known all that unless . . ."

Cal met my eyes.

"The house is bugged," we said in unison.

CHAPTER FOURTEEN

"The house being bugged makes perfect sense, because Austin and I had a conversation about our exact whereabouts this afternoon," I said. "On Sunday, anyone who was eavesdropping could've heard my reaction to the beef-heart prank and would know Holden's note called me a heartbreaker. Yesterday, Brandi told Preston and me she'd taken the job and would be starting on Wednesday, so whoever was listening would've known she'd be at work and could've stolen a sticky note."

"I'm so creeped out right now," Brandi said.

"Same." Ashley wrapped her arms around her waist.

"With all the technology available, it's not difficult to bug somebody's house, and this person has already proven he or she is tech savvy enough to get around your security system and video doorbell," Cal said. "We'll do a sweep to check."

I rubbed the goosebumps on my arms. How long had someone been listening to my private conversations? "Maybe when this person heard how we overreacted to Holden's prank, he or she decided to have some fun by toying with my mind—before killing me."

"Oh, hon, that's an awful thought," Ashley wailed.

The color drained from Cal's face. "Let's not jump to conclusions. Still, I'd rather you didn't go home tonight—even if Preston is with you."

"He'll want to stay at the hospital with Austin," I said. "I can stay with—"

"Come to my parents' house," Brandi said. "My mom will love it. It'll be like the slumber parties I had in high school."

I wasn't in a party mood, but it sounded better than dealing with my mom and Dan. "All right. I'll have J.T. keep Gus for the night."

Ashley smiled. "J.T. loves having Gus so much that he's already talking about getting a dog after we get married."

Then it was settled.

Brandi's mom, Patty, had popcorn and freshly baked sugar cookies waiting for us as soon as we arrived at her home on the outskirts of Wildcat Springs, so Brandi hadn't been kidding when she'd said it'd be like a slumber party.

"If you girls want to camp out here in the basement like Brandi and her high school friends used to, you can." Patty's eyes twinkled. "Or we have plenty of beds ready to go."

"Beds would be good, Mom." Brandi rested her hand on her lower back. "I can't take sleeping on the floor."

"I'll let you make room assignments. Your dad and I will be upstairs if you need us." She smiled. "You girls have a good time. As you can see, we have plenty of old movies on DVD—or VHS." She pointed to the oak entertainment center and headed upstairs with a bounce in her step that made her seem younger than her sixty-odd years.

"You *did* tell your parents what's going on, didn't you, hon?" Ashley stroked her cat's head.

"Yes," Brandi said. "Mom's trying to get everyone's minds off of what's happening and make us comfortable."

"Like you do." I dropped onto the puffy tan sectional and hugged a throw pillow to my chest. "I see where you get your knack for hospitality."

Brandi perused the entertainment center's shelf. "Do you want to watch a movie?"

"I want to help Georgia figure out how someone might've planted a bug in her house," Ashley said. "Unless you'd rather not?" She released the cat who retreated to a far corner behind a treadmill—probably to get away from Brandi's dog that was running around sniffing furniture.

"I'm good with it." I glanced at my phone to make sure I hadn't missed a call from Cal.

Nothing.

"You may need to step outside on the porch to make a call," Brandi said. "Between the brick exterior and metal roof, this house is a fortress."

I did have a weak signal, so I set my phone on the coffee table. "I don't want to bother Cal. Let's talk about who could've bugged my house." I tried to sound more enthusiastic than I felt, but it was a C+ effort—at best.

Brandi walked to a closet while Gigi nipped at her bare feet. "I have the perfect thing for a visual." She opened the door, disappeared inside, and backed out dragging a red-trimmed easel chalkboard. "My mom kept this for my nieces and nephews. I used to play teacher with this when I was little."

"I bet your siblings loved that," Ashley said.

"My school was fun."

"Uh-huh." Ashley laughed. "For you."

With chalk in hand, Brandi faced us while Gigi sat beside her. "Let's think through this situation. The way I see it, there are three options if your house is bugged. Someone planted it when you invited him or her in your house, someone found your security code and has been using it to access your house at will, or someone is really good at getting past security systems without being detected." She jotted those possibilities while Gigi stood on her hind legs and pawed the chalkboard ledge.

"Time out," I said. "We can't keep referring to this psycho as *someone*. I've been using the nickname Wallpaper Bandit, but we need a new name that includes the casserole—and possibly the bug."

We fell silent as we were brainstorming.

"How about Evil Eavesdropper?" Brandi asked.

"Works for me, because this psycho is definitely evil." I studied the board. "The first option is creepy, because it could mean Evil Eavesdropper is someone I trust."

"Maybe not." Ashley picked up her phone and tapped her thumbs on it. "Have you hired a repair person lately?"

"No. Grandpa and I are pretty good at fixing things."

"Have you received any deliveries where someone could've concealed a bug on a decorative object or electronic device?" Brandi asked.

"Nope." I shook my head. "I ordered some new clothes last month, but they're stashed in my bedroom closet."

"Bible study would've been a good opportunity for Arden or Wolfe to plant a bug." Brandi tapped the chalk against her palm.

Or Hamlet. *No. Don't go there.*

"Let's look at the second option—Evil Eavesdropper has your old security code," Brandi said. "Besides Ashley and me, who had it?"

"Mom, Dan, and Grandpa Winston." I looked at my friends. "How'd I tell you my code?"

"When we were at your house last spring—after the twins stayed with you," Ashley said. "We were cleaning up after small group, and you told us you'd changed it because you didn't want Preston and Austin to access your house."

"If my house was already bugged, then Evil Eavesdropper might've heard, but to do that, he or she still would've needed access first." I hated considering the possibility someone had been spying on me that long, but maybe Cal wouldn't find anything, and we were worrying for nothing. "Did either of you write down the code?"

"No, hon." Ashley stretched her legs out on the couch. "I'm good at retaining numbers."

"I memorized it too," Brandi said. "It wasn't that hard because you used Gus's birthday, and I have his special day marked in my planner so I can give him a treat."

"The planner wasn't sitting out when Arden was in your house, was it?" Ashley asked.

"No. I keep it in my purse in my bedroom."

"Since I used a date, I made it too easy to guess," I said.

"It's possible," Brandi said. "But how many people know your dog's birthday?"

I was certain I'd mentioned it to Hamlet. "I don't know. Gus isn't even a year old, so I haven't celebrated anything yet and never posted on social media." I sighed. "I'm willing to bet my mom wrote it down." I was going to hold off asking until absolutely necessary.

"Ah-*ha!*" Ashley wiggled her phone. "I've been searching for how to get around a security system, and it says here that burglars sometimes dust a keypad for prints. When they see which four keys are used, they guess the code."

"And since I used a date, that would've been one of the first combinations Evil Eavesdropper guessed."

"That sounds logical," Brandi said.

"That means Evil Eavesdropper could truly be anyone who wanted to toy with me by creating a mystery to solve." I groaned. "Could we watch a movie? I can't deal with any more of this tonight."

Brandi set the chalk on the ledge and brushed the dust from her hands. "No problem."

The next morning, I awoke at a little past three. For a few seconds, I struggled to remember where I was, and I sat up and looked around with my heart thudding.

I was at Brandi's parents' house in her sister Carly's old bedroom. I reached for my phone on the nightstand to see if Cal had texted. He hadn't. Out of habit, I checked the forecast for rain.

More sun and heat for days to come. My stomach knotted, and I groaned and dropped back onto the pillow. My crops desperately needed rain.

That was enough of a burden itself, but fear over what the day would bring at the hands of Evil Eavesdropper and guilt over my role in what'd happened to Austin nearly smothered me.

How stupid could I have been? Why didn't I consider the risk of putting my refrigerator in the garage? Why hadn't I realized someone could manually open the garage door? Probably because as creepy as the kitchen vandalism was, I didn't consider it deadly.

Or perhaps I'd allowed my happiness to cloud my judgment.

I'd thought that when Cal and I got back together, my world

had finally righted itself after months of upheaval, and we'd live happily ever after.

But was there such a thing as happily ever after?

Even though Cal had chosen to live without fear of something happening to me, I wondered if his original instinct had been correct. Was my mom right, and Cal and I *would* be better apart?

I drew the blanket to my chin and fought the rising panic until I recalled Brandi's admonition to put my hope in the Lord—and that I should read Psalm thirty-one.

I opened my Bible app. As I read the words of the Psalm, I soaked in the encouragement and made an effort to commit verse twenty-four to memory. *Be strong and take heart, all you who hope in the Lord.*

No wonder Brandi had pointed me to this chapter. She knew when I was spiraling.

"Lord, my hope is in you," I whispered. "Not in my circumstances. Not in Cal or our relationship. You alone." I stared at the ceiling and prayed until I drifted back to sleep.

Later that morning, I awoke, dressed, and went downstairs to eat the egg and sausage casserole Brandi's mom had prepared. After we finished breakfast, Brandi left for the high school, and Ashley went to her studio while I waited for Cal to pick me up and take me to the hospital to visit Austin. Cal's mom was on her way into town and planning to meet us there, and I was certain he'd enlisted her to be my babysitter until we found Evil Eavesdropper.

When Cal's work car pulled into the driveway, I hugged Patty, thanked her for her hospitality, and hurried out to meet him. The blazing sunshine and blue sky did little to improve my sober mood, and guilt about our fight the night before washed over me when I observed the dark circles rimming his eyes and his unshaven face.

I fastened my seatbelt. "You look exhausted."

"I'm fine. Just tired." He leaned over and kissed me. "How are you holding up?"

"I feel better than I did last night." I swallowed. "And I'm sorry for getting mad at you."

"I'm not trying to pick on Hamlet. I like him too, but—"

"You have to do your job."

"Yes." He backed out of the driveway onto the road.

I ran my finger along the edge of my seatbelt. I wanted to ask about the bug sweep, but part of me didn't want to know that someone had been listening to my private conversations. "You found a bug, didn't you?"

"The smoke detector in your hallway had been replaced with a bug disguised as a detector, and there were two more listening devices hidden behind the workbenches in your garage and pole barn. All three take a SIM card and are voice activated, so the person who planted it is alerted when there's talking and can listen from a cell phone." He reached for my hand. "I'm sorry."

"Can you tell how long they've been there?"

"According to the manufacturer, they have about a two-week battery life on standby, and they were still functional. I'd guess they haven't been there more than a week." He tightened his grip on the steering wheel. "There were also GPS trackers on both of your vehicles."

I wanted to find a corner, eat chocolate, curl up in a ball, and never come out of hiding again. "Can you trace the equipment to find who purchased it?"

He drove toward Richardville. "We can try, but it won't be easy, because whoever took the time to plant the bugs and trackers would be careful not to leave a trail."

I wished I could disagree—but I couldn't.

Cal squeezed my other hand. "We'll figure this out."

That was the line he always used to comfort me, and I wanted to believe him. But how much worse would our situation get before we did?

When Cal and I reached the Richard County Hospital, his phone rang, so he found a parking space and answered. "Perkins." He listened and ran his fingers through his hair. "You've got to be kidding." He paused as the color drained from his face. "All right. I'll be there as soon as I can." He disconnected and slammed his fist against the steering wheel.

"What's wrong?" I whispered.

"Diana Graham was strangled to death with her dog's leash early this morning."

CHAPTER FIFTEEN

Hopelessness swelled over me as breakfast casserole churned in my stomach and threatened to reappear. I rested my hand on the car's window control switch and closed my eyes. "No. No. *No!* That poor woman."

"I know. I need you to keep that information to yourself until it's released to the public. I only told you because . . ."

"Right," I said quickly. "I won't say anything."

Diana's loved ones would be devastated. I stared out the window at the vehicles passing on the highway next to the hospital. My mind swirled as I tried to make sense of everything that'd happened, and my thoughts drifted to the limerick.

A mystery for Georgia Rae. Who'll jump right into the fray.

Had my habit of solving mysteries led to Diana's murder? Had Evil Eavesdropper killed her just to give me a mystery to solve?

"What if Evil Eavesdropper heard you tell me about the dog leash killer and murdered Diana that way as a part of this sick mystery game created for me?" I shuddered. "The original dog leash killer is dead, and now that we know that my house was bugged, it can't be a coincidence that someone would choose the same method to murder Diana."

"I agree—and it makes me sick."

"But why choose Diana?" I whispered. "Even if Evil Eavesdropper did intend to kill the twins with the casserole and had to go with a backup plan to get a dead body to create 'a mystery for Georgia Rae,' why choose someone I barely knew instead of murdering me or someone close to me who has a dog . . . like Brandi?" Saying those words aloud made my stomach clench, but we needed to consider all angles.

"Perhaps that was the plan, and Brandi staying at her parents' house last night saved her life." He glanced in the rearview mirror. "Or Evil Eavesdropper had an issue with Diana."

"And killed two birds with one stone?" I winced at my poor word choice.

"Something like that." He grimaced.

I considered Diana's flirtatious behavior. "The limerick said, 'Heartbreak can be cruel.' Maybe *she* broke someone's heart."

"That wouldn't surprise me. But whatever the killer's reason, I'm glad you'll be spending the day with my mom." He motioned to the black sedan pulling into the space next to us. "There she is."

His mother, Yvonne Conner, got out of the car, and we joined her. After divorcing Cal's father, she'd begun using her maiden name and dating a much younger man.

She wore a tight denim skirt, silver espadrille wedge sandals, and a bright yellow tank top that set off her dark hair. Yvonne hugged her son, and when she squeezed me, her vanilla perfume mingled with cigarette smoke.

"I knew you'd get back together with my son." She stepped back but kept her hands on my arms. "Then again, you may be having second thoughts after everything that's happened."

"No, ma'am."

"Enough with the *ma'am* garbage, Georgia Peach." She emitted her signature cackle-croak that I'd dubbed a croakle. "Yvonne's going to be your mother-in-law someday, and she's here to catch this psycho who's trying to ruin your lives."

My face flamed as I glanced at Cal, who was grinning. I didn't want to argue with her—mainly because I hoped she was right about me marrying Cal. However, I still wasn't too sure about having her as a mother-in-law.

"I need to get going," Cal glanced at his mom, and some sort of unspoken communication passed between them. "Love you both."

He kissed me, and when he got in his car and drove away, I fought the urge to chase it through the parking lot like a forlorn puppy. Instead, Yvonne and I entered the hospital, and when we stepped off the elevator on the second floor, she informed me she had an urgent phone call to make and would be in the waiting area down the hall from Austin's room.

I had a sneaking suspicion she was calling her son.

I dodged a food service worker pushing a cart of used breakfast trays full of gloppy oatmeal and greeted an elderly man walking with an IV pole before I located Austin's private room.

"Sissy!" Austin greeted me in a hoarse voice. He was propped up in bed but was paler than normal, and an IV remained in his arm.

Preston, wearing a shirt and tie, sat next to his brother's bed. "The doctor told Austin they're springing him this afternoon."

"That's great news." I perched on a chair in front of his bed and silently praised God for this positive development among the chaos.

"You didn't bring me flowers or even a measly smiley-face balloon? I'm crushed." Austin clutched his heart.

"I see you're nearly back to normal." I withdrew a gift card for his favorite sporting goods store from my purse and tossed it at him. "Will this do instead?"

He examined it. "You're the best."

"How're you feeling?" I asked.

"Physically, a little weak. Mentally, stupid for falling for that trick. I'm never eating mushrooms again."

"Don't feel stupid," I said. "The last time you stayed with me, Brandi brought food, so it's only natural that you'd think she did this time. The casserole *did* look good."

"Dude, I've had Brandi's cooking, so I would've chowed down," Preston said. "And don't forget she brought us cookies on Tuesday. Between the two of us, we ate like a dozen."

"Yeah. I suppose," Austin said. "Is your boyfriend any closer to catching the person who's behind all this stuff?"

I considered what I should say since talking about Diana was off limits. "He has some leads. Someone that I've been calling Evil Eavesdropper bugged my house and knew you guys were staying with me. We think you were targeted because of the timing of the delivery when I wouldn't be there to stop you from eating the casserole. It's possible the plan was to make you really sick, because if Evil Eavesdropper intended to kill you, he or she could've used a . . . more efficient type of poison."

The twins exchanged glances.

"That's twisted," Preston said. "And I commend you for your tact."

Austin nodded. "Totally. Here I was thinking I'd protected you like one of those food tasters for ancient kings when I needed a taster for myself."

I charged ahead with my next question before I could change my mind. "How are you doing . . . emotionally?" I wasn't convinced I'd get a straight answer, because talking to the twins about deep, personal feelings wasn't exactly our standard operating procedure. I looked back and forth at them, and they squirmed.

Austin couldn't meet my eyes. "This has been a huge wake-up call."

Preston fidgeted with his phone. "I can't imagine life without my bro."

"We've both been focusing on the wrong things ever since college. Money. Women. Having fun."

A while back, Preston had told me that they were trying to see who could make the most money to buy the biggest house with the best entertaining area first. "Focusing on the wrong thing is easy to do," I said. "We've all been guilty of doing that in some way or another."

"Preston's been getting more serious about God lately and going to church, but I've kept doing my own thing," Austin said. "I need to stop living for myself when I know God wants me to serve him."

"I've been praying about that," I said.

"You know us better than I realized." Austin shot a weak grin in my direction.

"What'd you expect?" Preston asked. "She's an awesome detective, and we aren't that hard to figure out."

"That's accurate, bro."

"But now I'm going to prove *we* know *you* better than you realize." Preston pointed at me.

Uh-oh. His psychoanalysis about my kitchen had been spot on—even if it *had* been said in jest.

"Right now, you're blaming yourself for what happened to Austy," Preston said. "You're thinking that if you hadn't let us stay with you that none of this would've happened."

I didn't bother to deny what was obviously true. I even felt somewhat responsible for Diana Graham's murder, even though the rational part of me knew that was ridiculous.

Austin crossed his arms. "You're trying to keep yourself together and be tough, but you're freaking out inside right about now."

"Pretty much." It didn't take a rocket scientist to figure that one out.

Preston looked me straight in the eyes. "I'm speaking for both of us when I say, don't you even think about, for one second, giving yourself up to this psycho."

The temperature in the room seemed to drop a good ten degrees. I wanted to tell him he was crazy, and I'd never do that. But if the circumstances were right, wouldn't I sacrifice myself to protect the people I loved?

What if that was Evil Eavesdropper's end game?

I swallowed. "But if—"

"No!" Austin shook his head. "Promise us, no matter how bad it gets, you won't let Evil Eavesdropper get into your head and convince you to do something rash."

I studied my hands, folding and unfolding them. Squeezing one hand over a fist.

"We're not kidding," Preston said. "Promise."

Under the cover of my left hand, I crossed two fingers on my right. "I promise."

CHAPTER SIXTEEN

"Let's go." Yvonne motioned for me to follow as soon as I left Austin's hospital room. "We've got things to do."

"What're we doing?" Even though my legs were much longer than hers, my flip-flops clicked a rapid tempo as I practically chased her down the hallway.

"You're going to help Yvonne get to the bottom of this mess." She stopped in front of the nurses' station and jabbed the elevator's call button. "While you were gabbing with your stepbrothers, I talked to Cal." She lowered her voice. "He told me about Diana Graham."

So my instincts had been right. I was glad I didn't have to keep that information from her. "Where are—?"

"Tell me about Hamlet Miller." The elevator dinged, and she stepped inside.

I followed her. "Why?"

"Humor me."

There was no point in arguing, and I wasn't sure what she already knew. The elevator slid closed.

"He's an actor but moved home to Wildcat Springs earlier

this year because he thought he wanted to quit acting and flip houses. After a while, he missed acting and is restarting his career with a role in a local musical and an upcoming indie film in Chicago."

"Why'd you break up?"

"I couldn't follow him to Chicago or New York or wherever and keep farming."

"Did you love him?"

The doors parted, and we walked through the lobby and past the gift shop.

"As a friend." This had to top the list of subjects never to discuss with your boyfriend's mother.

"Did he love you?"

"Not enough to stay in Wildcat Springs," I said. "Just like I didn't love him enough to follow him."

We marched outside toward her car. I blinked in the sun, so I dug through my purse, fished out my sunglasses, and slipped them on.

"How'd he take the breakup?"

"Fine. It was mutual."

"You sure?" She opened her car door. "He *is* an actor, after all."

"I'm positive." As I got into the car, I was nearly overcome by the smell of stale, hot cigarette smoke lingering in the upholstery. "Hamlet wouldn't hurt me, if that's what you're getting at." I glanced at Yvonne out of the corner of my eye, and it was obvious she wasn't buying it.

"That's exactly what I'm getting at. He might've been aware that his brother left you that creepy note that called you a heart-breaker. He saw your kitchen was outdated. He had opportunity to bug your house and could've guessed your security code was your dog's birthday. Am I right?"

"Yes. I mentioned Gus's birthday to him, because I give the

dog a treat every month on the fourth, and I talked about how I'd have to do something big for his first birthday in September."

"He knows you like what he did with Cal's kitchen and could've stripped your wallpaper, so you had no choice but to turn to him for help when he offered." She snapped her seatbelt. "Then, he could be near you."

"I don't think—"

"He had access to the sticky notes in your buddy's house this week."

"What?" My heart squeezed to a temporary stop. No wonder Brandi had turned pale when I'd mentioned that Cal suspected Hamlet. "Brandi didn't say anything about that to me."

"Seems she just remembered Hamlet stopped by her house on Tuesday evening to borrow her ice cream maker. She texted Cal early this morning, though he didn't tell me that you didn't know." She cranked the engine and air conditioner.

I was going to give him the benefit of the doubt and assume he figured that Brandi had already told me since I'd been with her. But why hadn't *Brandi* mentioned that detail? Did she truly suspect her cousin, or did she not want me to worry?

"Please stop." My stomach twisted. "Hamlet would never hurt me—or poison anyone to get back at me for our relationship not working out."

"I know that's what you *want* to believe, but Cal told me Hamlet has a possible motive to kill Diana Graham—since she was bad-mouthing him and his business and made him lose out on a date with her sister Arden." Yvonne zoomed through the parking lot.

Why had I repeated to Cal what Hamlet had told me yesterday? "There's absolutely no way he would've killed Diana. Besides, they're not going to be business competitors for much longer since he's moving, and he decided it was fine that things didn't work out with Arden." I tried to sound certain, but doubts crept into my mind.

"Your loyalty's admirable. The trouble is, in all my years as a homicide detective I've witnessed things you wouldn't believe, and the one thing I've seen over and over is that jealousy does strange things to people. That, and people are good at hiding their dark sides." She hit the brakes for a red light.

"But my breakup with Hamlet was mutual!" How many times did I have to say it?

"You didn't wait very long after breaking up with him to get back with Cal."

She and Bobbi Sue were soul sisters. "I was still in love with Cal."

"I know. That's an observation—not a criticism. It's also the type of situation that might cause a heartbroken young man to do strange things."

I gritted my teeth. "I've known Hamlet Miller for years because he was my brother's best friend in high school. I've never known him to be anything but kind and thoughtful. Even if he was heartbroken, lost his mind, and stooped to stripping my wallpaper so I'd have to hire him for a renovation so he could have an excuse to be around me, there's nothing in me that believes that he'd bug my house, poison my stepbrother, or kill Diana Graham. There's not even a single thing about him that ever gave me an uneasy feeling. Ever!"

Yvonne pursed her lips. "All right. Your gut counts for something. But I'm still going to keep an eye on Hamlet—and everyone else in your life. If this person is responsible for killing Diana Graham, then we have to consider every possibility. And that person is very likely someone you trust."

"Or it's someone I don't know—like the person who killed Natalie Thrailkill."

"Maybe so. But why would Natalie's murderer kill Diana Graham?"

That was the big question that I needed to answer—for my own safety and for Hamlet's future. "I don't know."

"Georgia Peach, I truly think the person behind these shenanigans is someone who knows you well."

I didn't have the strength to keep arguing with her. "Are you going to tell me where we're headed?"

"The first stop is for food. Yvonne's hungry. Then we're going to the airport to pick up Mason Thrailkill since Cal can't do it himself."

While Yvonne and I had eaten lunch at an outdoor café in Richardville, she'd told me plenty of entertaining stories about Cal as a kid. My favorite was about the time when he was ten and he and two boys on his baseball team were upset because someone had sprayed graffiti on the dugout at their diamond. They dubbed themselves private investigators and went around their neighborhood asking witnesses what they'd seen and heard. The police pegged a pair of juvenile delinquents first, but Cal and his buddies *had* helped locate an elderly woman's lost Dachshund, Willie, so they'd considered their mission a success.

Now we were sweltering in the parking lot next to the terminal at Richardville Executive Airport with the car turned off and the windows open because Yvonne hated to waste gas.

"When you said we were picking up Mason at the airport, I thought you meant Indianapolis International." Sweat dribbled down my back as I fanned my T-shirt away from my body and hoped she'd get the hint.

"Mason has his private pilot's license." Yvonne lit a cigarette, took a drag, and held it out the window. "His parents were well off, and they died when he was a kid, so he got the whole kit and caboodle when he came of age. From what I've gathered, his grandma is loaded too." She croaked. "Otherwise, we both know he wouldn't be able to afford a plane on a cop's salary."

The terminal's glass door slid open, and a pudgy woman lumbered outside followed by Wolfe Sommers. What was he doing here?

"Yvonne," I whispered and pointed. "That's Wolfe Sommers. He was on a lunch date with Diana the other day. He asked me out last Saturday, and I said *no*. He was even in my house for small group on Sunday." I didn't think it was necessary to mention Hamlet had invited him.

"Hmm." She peered over the top of her oversized sunglasses. "I wonder who that lady is. His granny?"

Wolfe led the older woman across the parking lot toward a gray sedan. I sat up straighter. "A car like that one almost side-swiped me last Sunday when I was on my way to church."

"There are a lot of gray sedans on the road."

"Driven by a man I've rejected?"

"Fair enough." She blew smoke out of the car.

But hadn't I seen Wolfe leave Latte Conspiracies and get into a white convertible on Saturday? Why was he driving a gray car now? Before I could think better of it, I unbuckled my seatbelt, launched myself out, and jogged across the parking lot. Since the Almighty had placed Wolfe in my path, I figured it was my duty to talk to him.

"Wolfe!" I waved.

Holding onto the car door, he displayed his game-show host grin. "Georgia. Nice to see you."

"We keep running into each other."

"Funny, isn't it?" He ducked inside, cranked the engine, and popped back out. "This is Liza Bell. She owns Bell's Dinner Theater and flew in for tonight's performance of *The Music*

Man." He motioned toward the woman sitting in the car. She had her phone pressed to her ear and wiggled her fingers at me.

"I see." I pointed to the vehicle, and my eyes fell on the Michigan license plate. What if he was borrowing Arden's car? "Did you get a new car?"

"Nope. Rental. My MX-5's in for repairs—undriveable," Wolf said. "Some idiot rear-ended poor Margie last night."

"Margie?"

He shrugged. "I always name my cars. I thought Margie Mazda sounded cute. I like alliteration."

Alliteration—a poetic device. Except the limerick on my kitchen wall hadn't used alliteration.

His gaze skittered away, and he focused on a red and white single-engine plane emerging from a hangar. "We'd better get going. Liza has some people she needs to meet before the show."

I couldn't let him escape—yet. "By the way, how was your lunch date with Diana Graham?"

Surprised flitted through his expression, but I couldn't determine if it was because of guilt—or because of my nosiness.

"She's nice enough, but I'm not into older women." He shoved his hands into his cargo shorts. "She likes to flirt with me at Latte Conspiracies, so when she asked me to lunch, I didn't tell her no because she's kinda interesting, and I never turn down a free meal. Working in a coffee shop and acting haven't exactly made me rich."

That was the most honest thing I'd ever heard Wolfe say.

"Then I found out she's Arden's older sister, and now I've blown any chance of ever getting Arden to change her mind about me." He sounded like a forlorn little boy.

"Why's that?" I wanted to see what he'd say.

"Because even though Diana and I don't have much in common, I can tell she's into me." He glanced at Liza, who was still on the phone, and then lowered his voice. "Diana sent me a selfie the other night and—let's just say Jesus wouldn't be happy." His cheeks tinged pink.

I didn't care to dwell on *that* revelation. "I've heard Arden and her sister don't get along, so she might not care about girl code."

"Really?" Hope dawned in his expression, and his Wolfe Sommers persona made a comeback. "Then I'll have to keep using my charms to convince her."

"Hold on," I said. "Maybe instead of being Wolfe Sommers the actor, you should focus on being Wolfe Sommers the *friend* and see what happens."

"That's brilliant. Arden would dig Wendall!"

"Wendall?"

"My real first name. Don't know what my parents were thinking. I was this nerdy little kid with glasses who got bullied all the time. When I became an actor, I picked a name that sounded tough and became *Wolfe*." He squared his shoulders, then glanced into the car. "I'd better go. See you around, Georgia."

Unless he was spinning a story to throw me off his track, then he wasn't Chuck Richman's cousin Travis out for revenge. But that didn't mean he wasn't somehow involved in tormenting me—for another reason.

"Take care." I returned to Yvonne's car.

"Well?" she asked as I got in.

"Wolfe was here to pick up the owner of Bell's Dinner Theater, and he claims the gray car is a rental because he had an accident. I asked him about his lunch date with Diana to see how he'd react at the mention of her name, and I don't think he has any idea she's dead. But he *is* an actor, so he could've fooled me."

"So's your ex-boyfriend, and he has more reasons to want revenge."

I literally had to bite my tongue.

"Anything else?" Yvonne asked.

"Wolfe's real name is Wendall."

"How'd that come up?"

I told her. "For a while, I thought it was possible Wolfe was Chuck Richman's cousin Travis since Wolfe is from Florida, but I guess that theory's wrong. Unless Wolfe was lying about his real name."

"Does seem convenient he fed you that line about Wendall the Kid Nerd."

My stomach tightened. "I did ask Hamlet if *Wolfe Sommers* was his stage name, so . . ."

"You think Hamlet mentioned that to Wolfe."

"He might've, since they work together."

Yvonne honked and waved at a nice-looking, but gaunt, blond man emerging from the terminal. He appeared to be carrying more weight than just the backpack slung over one of his shoulders. She stuck her head out the window as he approached. "Good to see you again, Mason." She hitched her thumb back at me. "This is Cal's Georgia."

Cal's Georgia. I liked that.

He dumped his backpack onto the seat and got in. "You're even prettier than your picture." His smile was sincere, but his voice carried a weary note.

"I like you already," I said.

"Cal was sorry he couldn't meet you himself, but he's investigating a homicide in Wildcat Springs." Yvonne exited the parking lot onto the county road.

"He's had his hands full ever since he moved here." Mason buckled his seatbelt. "When he left Cleveland, he thought he'd have a slower pace in Richard County."

"Crime is everywhere, son." Yvonne glanced in the rearview mirror. "People have all kinds of dirty secrets in these little towns. Did my boy give you the scoop about what's been happening to Georgia?"

"No, but he alluded to something that he wanted to talk to me about." His forehead creased in concern. "What's going on?"

"Give him the low down, Georgia," Yvonne said.

"It all began with a beef heart." I told him about Holden's prank and why the ornery teenager had left the package. "Then, some sicko we've been calling the Evil Eavesdropper figured out how to get around my security system, tore off my kitchen wallpaper, and wrote a limerick on the wall that indicated he or she was creating a mystery for me to solve. Unless Holden was working with someone, he couldn't have done it because he has an alibi." I opened the picture on my phone and held it so he could see the poem.

The line between Mason's eyebrows deepened as he studied the photo.

"My stepbrothers Austin and Preston came to protect me, and Evil Eavesdropper put a poisoned casserole in my refrigerator with a note that appeared to be from one of my best friends. Austin ate some and is now in the hospital being treated for muscarine poisoning."

A look of horror spread across Mason's face. "What's his prognosis?"

"Thankfully, he'll be fine," I said. "Oh, and if that wasn't enough, we figured out my house was bugged."

"Does Cal have any leads?"

"She left out the worst part." Yvonne glanced at me. "Go ahead. Tell him about Diana Graham."

I fidgeted with my seatbelt. "A few days ago, before Cal and I knew Holden was responsible for the beef heart, we were fearful that the person who killed Natalie might be coming after me. While we were discussing that, Cal told me how Chuck Richman was falsely accused, went to prison, and died before you and Cal found evidence to exonerate him. Cal said you think one of

Chuck's family members or friends might've killed Natalie for revenge."

He nodded. "Right."

"We also talked about the possibility that the pranks had nothing to do with the Chuck Richman case and that the person responsible might be someone we know from Wildcat Springs. This morning, one of the people we suspected locally, Diana Graham, was found dead," I said.

"Strangled with her dog's leash," Yvonne added.

Mason grimaced. "And since your house was bugged, you think Evil Eavesdropper may have listened to you and Cal talking, wrote the limerick and vandalized your kitchen, poisoned your stepbrother, and killed Diana just to give you a mystery to solve?"

"Yes," I said. "Now that Diana's dead, it's unlikely the pranks have anything to do with someone avenging Chuck Richman . . . since Cal told me that no one vandalized your house or threatened Natalie prior to her murder."

"That's true." Mason closed his eyes and squeezed the bridge of his nose. "I was going to wait for Cal to share this news, but clearly, I need to put your mind at ease." He met my gaze. "My buddy called about an hour ago and told me they arrested a guy for Natalie's murder this morning."

CHAPTER SEVENTEEN

My eyes widened. "Mason, that's great!"

"It is, but it won't bring her back, and my son still has to grow up without his mother." Mason swallowed. "I just hope this guy's convicted because he needs to be put away for life for what he did to Nat."

"Sure does," Yvonne muttered.

We rode in silence until I couldn't hold in my question any longer. "What're you allowed to tell us?"

Mason stared out the window as we crossed the bridge over Wildcat Creek. "The alleged serial killer's name is Tab Wilson," Mason said. "Two days ago, he murdered a young woman who was biking alone on a trail."

"Like Natalie," I whispered.

"Right. Only this time, probably because it's summer instead of the middle of winter, a witness saw Tab fleeing and gave a vehicle description. The detectives pieced together CCTV footage and found his car. When they got a warrant to search his house, they found the victim's missing earring." Mason swallowed hard. "They also found Natalie's missing earring and pictures of her."

I shivered. "Has Tab killed anyone else?"

"No, but from all the pictures of women biking alone, he was clearly planning to." He ran his finger over his bag. "I begged Natalie not to ride by herself, because I was afraid something would happen to her. She thought I was just a cynical cop and refused to live in fear. Back in February we had a few days of warmer weather, and she was determined to get out and enjoy them before we got more snow." He gazed out the car window. "And you know the rest of that story."

"What about the letter you received?" I asked.

He emitted a wry chuckle. "Turns out, Nat's murder had nothing to do with the Chuck Richman case that Cal and I botched. The detectives found a copy of the note I received on Tab's computer. They think when he realized Natalie was a detective's wife, he wrote the letter and planted it in my gym locker to confuse the investigation—and it worked."

"So all this time, Cal's been worrying for no reason." I slumped against my seat.

"Yeah." Mason shook his head. "He certainly has."

"Or not," Yvonne said. "Because even though this case has nothing to do with what happened to Natalie, somebody close to home is still out to get you, Georgia Peach."

Late that evening, Mason, Yvonne, and I gathered at Cal's house for dinner after he got off work. I'd asked Brandi to join us, thinking she might be interested in meeting Mason, but she'd declined because she was too tired from her new job and wanted to go to bed early.

We sat outside on Cal's patio as the sun set, and a gentle

breeze swirled around us while the smell of tasseled corn hung in the air. Miss Peacock rested under the table as we ate grilled steaks, corn on the cob, and green beans from my garden. After we finished, the conversation turned to Evil Eavesdropper.

"We confirmed the mushrooms in the casserole are a common type of poisonous mushroom," Cal said.

"What about the sticky note?" Yvonne sipped water from a sweaty glass.

"There was a partial print of Brandi's on the note, which is no surprise, but the casserole container was clean," Cal said. "Vanessa spoke with Brandi's neighbors, but none of them witnessed anyone entering Brandi's house or heard her dog barking. However, the neighbors to the north are on vacation, and the house to the south is for sale—and vacant."

"Which makes Arden look even guiltier, since she was at Brandi's house a couple of days ago," I said.

Cal met my gaze. "Hamlet was there too."

I decided to ignore that statement. "Diana asked Wolfe on a date," I said. "If Arden was interested in Wolfe, maybe she was mad about her sister getting in on her territory, which gives her motive. She's tall and thin and could be the female jogger that Jerry Fincher and Lorelei McPherson saw around the time my wallpaper was stripped. Pastry Delight was closed because she was sick, but she could've been faking." I looked back and forth at Mason and Yvonne. "Don't forget, Lorelei thought it was weird that the jogger had her kid covered with a blanket since it was hot."

"Or the mystery runner really was a mom trying to protect her baby from the sun. We don't know that she had anything to do with the wallpaper." Cal crossed his arms. "Hamlet could've parked behind your barns while he was vandalizing your kitchen."

"Hamlet wouldn't kill anyone!" I shouted.

Yvonne and Mason exchanged glances.

"We ran into Wolfe today when we were at the airport," Yvonne said. "Tell Cal about it, Georgia."

Thankful for Yvonne's intervention, I did. "Obviously, I didn't say anything about Diana's murder, but I did ask about their lunch date, and the mention of her name didn't bother him —though he did turn red thinking about the selfie she'd sent him." I looked at Cal. "I don't suppose you can tell us any more details about her case."

"No."

We sat in silence as the birds chirped and locusts buzzed, and we needed a more lighthearted topic.

"Mason," I said. "Yvonne was telling me some stories about Cal as a kid this afternoon. Do you have any good tales?"

Mason laughed. "What's it worth to you for me to keep my mouth shut, Perkins?"

"You're dreaming if you think you're getting a dime from me." Cal dimpled. "I don't keep secrets from Georgia."

"Don't say I didn't warn you." Mason leaned back and steepled his fingers. "Back when Cal made detective in Cleveland, he and I were both bachelors and decided to try the online dating thing. Have you ever done that?"

"Yes," I said. "I struck out. Big time."

"It worked for me," Yvonne said.

"Casanova here was inundated with women chasing him and was scheduling multiple dates every weekend." Mason pointed at Cal.

"I had a lot of coffee and dinner dates," Cal said. "I wasn't hitting it off with anyone."

We'd talked about our lousy online dating experiences, so I had a feeling he was saying that more for his mom's benefit than mine.

"He's picky," Mason said.

"He was holding out for quality." Yvonne winked at me.

I appreciated her support.

"Anyway, one Friday night, I had a first date with a girl I'd been talking to for several weeks." Mason picked up a napkin ring and spun it on his finger. "We met at a pizza place and clicked, so we shared some of our online dating experiences. Turns out, she'd been on an extremely interesting coffee date that very afternoon."

"Uh-oh," I said.

"Uh-oh is right." Cal's eyes twinkled.

"She was getting coffee with this guy named Cal, who was nice enough, but right in the middle of the date, a woman came flying up to their table and demanded to know why he hadn't called her back after their date and why he had the nerve to bring woman after woman into her shop to taunt her."

"Oh, man." I groaned.

"I never told Daphne I'd call," Cal said. "The last thing I said was 'Nice to meet you,' which everyone knows is code for 'We survived one date, but there's not going to be a second.'"

"Obviously everyone except Daphne knows," Mason said.

Yvonne lit a cigarette. "What'd you tell her, son?"

"I apologized for giving her the wrong impression and told her I wasn't aware it was her shop, which made her even more upset, because apparently, I hadn't listened to her on our date—or recognized her when she was working. But she'd dyed her hair blonde and cut it short."

Mason guffawed. "As good of a detective as you are, you can be blind when it comes to women, Perkins."

Yvonne croakled.

Mason's statement was accurate, but out of loyalty to Cal, I'd never agree—out loud. "Then what happened?"

"She kicked Natalie and me out of the shop," Cal said.

"Wait." I looked at Mason. "Natalie who was your wife, Natalie?"

"Yep." He grinned. "It's lucky for me Daphne came along and discouraged Nat, or Cal might've beaten me out."

"No way." Cal chuckled. "We had a nice time, but you and Natalie were perfect for each other."

Mason squeezed his eyes shut. "I know."

CHAPTER EIGHTEEN

The night before, we'd decided the safest place for me to stay was Cal's guest room because of the presence of three people who either had or currently worked in law enforcement. Gus was still with J.T., and my cousin assured me my canine buddy was safe and having a good time.

Friday morning, Mason was eager to get home to his son, so after Cal left for work, Yvonne and I took him to the airport so he could fly back to Atlanta.

"What now?" I asked Yvonne as Mason waved goodbye and entered the terminal. I was fairly certain Yvonne didn't want to tag along while I mowed side ditches or hauled grain.

"You tell me. Now that we know Evil Eavesdropper is somebody close to home, and Diana's murder has hit the news, we could poke around a little and try to figure out what happened to her." She backed up, but the car's warning system dinged as a burgundy truck blazed into her path.

Yvonne slammed the brakes as Jerry Fincher stuck his head and arm out of the truck window and gave us the middle finger before honking and roaring out of the parking lot.

"That was rude, crude, and socially unacceptable," Yvonne snapped.

"No kidding. He's my neighbor."

"He got something against you?"

I told her about the school board election and the Dillman farm.

She narrowed her eyes and drove out of the lot. "Hmph. I'll tell Cal to take a closer look at him."

"I don't know if Jerry knew Diana Graham, but seeing if there's a connection can't hurt because he certainly doesn't like me." I was glad she was considering someone other than Hamlet as a suspect.

"Now. As I was about to ask before your idiot neighbor nearly ran us over, when you've gone snooping in the past, what do you do?"

"Try to stay out of harm's way and talk to people in town who are in the know."

"Like Bobbi Sue in that kooky little coffee shop."

I stifled a groan. *Life Lesson #1589: Avoid interactions that include your ex-boyfriend's mother and your current boyfriend's mother.* "She's an excellent source."

"Then that's where we'll go. You can't convince me she hasn't heard something about Diana Graham working in that shop of hers."

"But you suspect her son Hamlet is guilty."

"Unless you told her, she doesn't know."

Yvonne was right, and I knew it. I just didn't want to face Bobbi Sue with Yvonne in tow. On second thought, I didn't want to face Bobbi Sue while Yvonne towed *me* along.

"Does Cal know you're doing this?" I asked.

"Protecting you?"

"Investigating."

She snorted. "If he didn't want me to, then he should've told me not to come visit."

That didn't quite answer my question.

Ten minutes later, we found a parking space in the public lot, because the portion of Main Street in front of Latte Conspiracies had been closed for the Wildcat Arts Festival. Workers were setting up tents and food booths between Pearl Street and Park Road. When we entered the coffee shop, only one man staring at a laptop was seated in the corner. At least there would only be a single witness to spread gossip if things went bad.

"Georgia! Yvonne!" Bobbi Sue greeted me with a huge smile. "Good to see you again. What can I get for you?"

At least she appeared to have forgiven me for my transgression of not keeping Hamlet in Wildcat Springs. "Iced Moon Landing Mocha."

"Yvonne doesn't do fussy drinks. Coffee—black." She handed Bobbi Sue some money. "I'm buying Georgia's."

"What are you ladies doing today?" Bobbi Sue asked as she made change.

"We're having a girls' day," Yvonne said.

That was one way of putting it.

"Awww, isn't that sweet. Are you going to the arts festival?" Bobbi Sue pointed out the window.

"We haven't gotten that far with our planning, but that sounds interesting," Yvonne said.

"I'm working at my friend Ashley's booth tomorrow, and you're welcome to join me."

Bobbi Sue poured Yvonne's coffee and handed it to her. "You'll need something to keep busy while your son's occupied investigating Diana Graham's death."

"That's right," Yvonne said.

"It's awful about Diana, and it's all anyone's talking about this morning. Makes me glad the hubs and I have cats because I wouldn't want to be walking a dog at night around here." Bobbi Sue grabbed a cup for my drink. "Although, it's completely possible Diana just ticked off the wrong person, and the rest of us folks don't have anything to worry about."

Now we were getting somewhere. I glanced at Yvonne, who nodded ever-so-slightly. "How so?" I asked.

"She had a way about her that rubbed a lot of people wrong. She could appear sweet and nice and then turn and stab you in the back." Bobbi Sue handed me my drink. "I have a new employee named Wolfe, and some of the older ladies think he's a hoot. Makes them feel young again when he teases them. A couple of weeks ago, Diana was in here, saw him flirting with Taryn Anderson, and got all bent out of shape. Diana brought it to my attention so I could speak to him, because she didn't want me to lose customers." Bobbi Sue rolled her eyes.

"What'd Wolfe say?" I asked.

"He admitted flirting, and I even talked to Taryn. She wasn't upset and told me all he'd done was ask for her phone number. I told him not to do that while he was working and figured the whole thing was over."

Wolfe had obviously taken his boss's admonition with a grain of salt.

"The next thing I know," Bobbi Sue continued, "I'm hearing rumors that Diana is telling anyone who'll listen that the naughty barista at Latte Conspiracies is a—and I quote—'lady killer' and that young girls should keep their distance."

Yvonne choked, and I would've too if I'd had a mouthful of mocha.

"Turns out, she was trying to get rid of her younger competition so she could be" —Bobbi Sue leaned closer and lowered her voice— "a cougar."

"Some women like younger men." Yvonne's eyes twinkled.

Yes. Yes, they did.

Bobbi Sue directed her gaze at Yvonne. "But they don't have to be obnoxious about it."

"Fair enough," Yvonne said. "Did she happen to have her sights set on Hamlet?"

Inwardly, I cringed. I needed to redirect this line of questioning before Bobbi Sue's paranoia kicked in, and she shut down.

"No, though my son is quite a catch." Bobbi Sue bristled. "Now if that's—"

"Can you think of anyone who might have had it out for Diana?" I asked quickly.

"Sure can," Bobbi Sue said. "You ever met Arden Tanner?"

"I have." I didn't think it was necessary to add that Arden wasn't the president of the Georgia Rae Winston Fan Club. I glanced at Yvonne, whose serious expression reminded me of Cal's game face when he was working.

"Word around town has it that Diana wanted to help Arden, so she convinced Arden to move here from Michigan. She lives in one of Diana's rental properties," Bobbi Sue said.

"Why'd Diana feel like she needed to help Arden?"

Bobbi Sue leaned forward and whispered, "Rumor has it, Arden needed to get away from an ex-boyfriend."

"You know any more details about that?" Yvonne asked.

"No, but it makes sense that Arden would turn to family."

"Do you have any idea why Arden might have had it out for Diana?" I had a few ideas, but I wanted Bobbi Sue's take.

"Allegedly, Diana's idea of helping was all about control. She wanted Arden to work for her interior design company, so she could mold her, but Arden had her own ideas and got a job working for Taryn at Pastry Delight. I heard she thought that job would give her more time to write her mystery novel."

"The nerve." I swirled the ice cubes in my mocha and took a sip.

Bobbi Sue walked around the counter and began straightening a shelf of alien-themed coffee mugs. "It sounds unbelievable, but Diana didn't like to be told no."

"I experienced that. She came up to me on the street and basically told me I'd be playing the piano at Cal's church for the service on Sunday."

"That's another thing," Bobbi Sue said. "Diana was telling everyone that Arden choked while playing the piano for the service, but Arden was in here with Taryn not that long ago. I was cleaning tables and overheard Arden tell Taryn the keys were sticking so badly she *couldn't* play. She admitted to getting frustrated and walking off, but she thought her sister had sabotaged the piano on purpose."

Interesting. I hadn't noticed a single key sticking, but they could've been repaired after Arden had complained. "Did Arden say if Diana was going to have the keys fixed?"

"No. But she was convinced Diana was trying to ruin her chances of playing."

After what Diana had told me herself, I couldn't exactly rule out that possibility. There weren't many people around who tuned pianos, so a few phone calls would tell me if the church's piano had been fixed recently.

"Do Arden and Taryn hang out a lot?"

"I don't know. I've only seen them together once."

I glanced at Yvonne who was tapping her foot, which I took to mean she was ready to split. "You've been helpful—as usual."

Bobbi Sue's eyes gleamed. "Enjoy your girls' day."

There was still a teeny-tiny bit of venom in the statement—but only someone who knew her well would've noticed.

Yvonne and I left the shop and walked back toward her car.

"What do you think?" I asked.

"We should talk to Taryn and get some piano tuners on the horn."

"Agreed." I finished my drink and tossed the cup into a cardboard trashcan next to a tent. "Are you hungry?"

"After chugging that sugar bomb of a mocha, you're telling me you are?" She surveyed me and lit a cigarette.

I tried not to feel judged since she was a lot thinner than I could ever dream of being, but that was currently about as likely as it was that I wasn't going to smell like cigarette smoke.

"Yes," I said with as much dignity as I could muster. "*Hungry* is code for the need to visit Pastry Delight in search of information, and any time I ply small business owners for information, I feel a moral obligation to patronize their stores."

"I wouldn't feel obligated to that hussy of a bakery owner who tried to steal my man, but whatever helps you sleep at night." She blew out a puff of smoke. "Cal's always liked curvy women, so don't you worry. I'll split a cookie with you. You pick the kind."

Split a cookie? I gazed at the sky. *Jesus, if you'd like to come riding on one of those puffy white clouds right about now, I'm A-okay with that.*

I led the way into Pastry Delight, where Taryn, who *hadn't* taken a head-first tumble into the Grand Canyon, waited behind the counter.

Nice Georgia.

"Hey, Taryn." I surveyed the pastry case. "Could I get an iced sugar cookie and two bottles of water?"

She opened the display. "I guess you made short work of that cookie tray Diana Graham gave you," she muttered.

I glanced at Yvonne, who was glaring at Taryn. "What cookie tray?" I asked.

"Diana bought an assorted cookie tray for you on Wednesday as a thank you for playing the piano at church. I guess she, uh, didn't get it to you before . . ." She handed me the cookie and water bottles. "Anyway . . . it's so sad about what happened."

"Yes. Is Arden here?" I asked. "I'd like to give her my condolences over the loss of her sister."

"Cut the crap, Georgia." Taryn's face darkened. "We both know you're here to snoop because Arden's at the sheriff's department being questioned about her sister's murder."

CHAPTER NINETEEN

No, no we both did *not* know that information. "I—"

"Now you listen here, Ms. Anderson. We're not paying our hard-earned money for your snippy attitude." Yvonne put her hands on her hips and leveled Taryn with a glare that would terrify even the most hardened criminals. "Is this how you treat all your customers?"

"No," Taryn mumbled as she took a step backward. "I'm sorry. No charge for the cookie and water."

"Thank you." I dropped my wallet back into my purse. "I really didn't know about Arden. Cal doesn't talk about ongoing investigations. Is she a suspect?"

"I don't know." Taryn cast a nervous glance at Yvonne. "When she called, she didn't give details except to say that she couldn't come to work because she was talking to the detectives."

"It's possible Cal wanted to question her to find out what she knew about Diana's life," I said.

"I hope so." Taryn smoothed her apron. "Arden may be a little different, but she's a hard worker. We've been getting along, and . . . I'd hate to think I hired a killer."

Yvonne and I glanced at each other.

"Do you have reason to believe she killed Diana?" Yvonne asked.

"I don't know." Taryn fidgeted with the pink bow on her apron. "Diana *was* gaslighting Arden."

"How so?" Yvonne edged closer.

"Like . . . when Arden moved here, she had a pet parakeet. She swore that Diana said pets, including birds, were allowed in her rental house. But when she got here, Diana told her she'd never given permission for her to have pets and that Arden had made up the entire conversation. Naturally, Arden didn't have it in writing because she didn't sign the lease until she got here and read where it specified no pets—of any kind. I tried to tell Arden that Diana was gaslighting her, but she wouldn't believe me and convinced herself that she'd misunderstood."

"Why do you think that is?" I asked.

"Arden loved and trusted her sister because she believed Diana was trying to help her through their mother's death and a bad break up."

"What happened to the bird?" I asked.

"She gave it to Lorelei McPherson."

Was it the same bird that'd perched on Lorelei's shoulder when Cal and I had talked to her? If Lorelei had adopted Arden's bird, wouldn't she have recognized Arden as the mystery runner with the legs that'd impressed Jerry Fincher? That meant if Arden had stripped my wallpaper, she wasn't the runner and might've concealed her vehicle behind my barns.

"Did Arden and Diana have any other conflicts besides the bird?" Yvonne asked.

"Diana made fun of Arden for wanting to be a mystery writer," Taryn said. "I overheard her say that Arden wasn't smart enough to write a novel."

"That's a brutal thing to say about your sister." I winced.

"Did Arden ever mention anything about an incident involving the church piano?"

Taryn nodded so vigorously her top knot wobbled. "The day she was asked to play, a bunch of keys were sticking. She got frustrated and walked out. Diana tried to convince her nothing was wrong with the piano—more gaslighting. I've heard Arden play, and she's really good. In fact, she's performing in the arts festival talent show tomorrow."

"Is it true that Diana convinced Arden to cancel a date with Hamlet Miller?" I asked.

"I'm not sure." Taryn smirked. "I do know Diana told Arden she didn't want to be the rebound relationship for a wannabe actor who was pining away for Georgia Rae Winston."

It might be time for boycott number two. I gritted my teeth.

"Diana thought Hamlet was stealing her design clients but whatever. It wasn't his fault she charged an arm and a leg for renovations and people wanted someone more affordable." Taryn shrugged and directed her gaze at me. "Hamlet's a nice guy but not a good match for Arden, and she knew it. If she'd been into him, she wouldn't have let Diana railroad her into cancelling."

Taryn made a good point because Arden had gone against Diana and gotten a job with Taryn. "Maybe Wolfe Sommers would be a better fit."

"Possibly." Taryn brushed her hand over the bakery case. "Look, I don't want to get Arden in any trouble just because she complained about a few issues with her overbearing sister."

"Fair enough," Yvonne said. "So let me ask you this. Do you have any idea who would've wanted to kill Diana?"

"No. I really didn't know her."

I looked at Yvonne, and she tilted her head toward the door, which I took to mean we were done with this little interrogation. We left the shop and piled into Yvonne's car.

"I'm glad Cal didn't get stuck with *her*," Yvonne said.

"He could still change his mind." I broke off my half of the cookie and held out the other piece.

"He won't." Yvonne waved the cookie away. "Go for it. You earned it after dealing with that perky little baker."

"Now what?" I stuffed a bite in my mouth, and the cookie practically melted. Maybe Taryn wasn't so bad after all.

"We let the professionals deal with Arden, and if they let her go, tomorrow we can track her down at that festival talent show Miss Perky Pants was talking about." She put the car in gear. "Right now, Yvonne needs to sit by your pond and work on her tan."

"You made an awful mess of this kitchen," Yvonne said as we entered my house.

"It has to get worse before it gets better." *Life Lesson #26.*

All the food in my refrigerator—which hadn't been much—had been removed, and Cal had ensured the appliance was returned to my kitchen.

She pushed aside the plastic and strode to my living room window. "You gonna join me out by the pond? You're a little on the pasty side."

I literally bit my tongue, because there was no point in lecturing a smoker on the dangers of skin cancer. "I'm going to call piano tuners to see if anyone worked on the church's piano, and then I need to haul grain to the elevator and weed my garden."

"You tell me when you're ready to go to the elevator, and I'll ride along. Farm life is fascinating."

"Will do." I provided a beach towel, and Yvonne headed outside.

Now that I was alone in my house, I felt Gus's absence more

than ever, but his safety was more important than my need for canine companionship.

I searched my phone for piano tuners in the area and called the first one on the list. He hadn't repaired the church piano, and it took two more tries before Jim—of Jim's Piano Service—came through.

"I took a look at Liberty Christian Church's piano—a couple of weeks ago," he said. "Is something wrong?"

"No. I played it last Sunday, and the keys were working beautifully, and the sound was great."

"Glad to hear it," Jim said. "The pastor told me someone complained about multiple keys sticking, but I only found one. There was a tiny piece of wood wedged between middle C and D. The wood piece was thin. Looked like a broken matchstick. Don't know why someone would be playing with matches around pianos, but I've seen strange things in my day. I reckon some kids escaped the Sunday school classrooms and were messing around."

"Was there anything else wrong?"

"Nope. Once I took the wood piece out, the piano was fine."

I thanked Jim for his help, disconnected, and went into my bedroom to change into work clothes.

It was certainly possible that Diana had deliberately sabotaged the piano and then missed a piece while fixing it—just to ruin her sister's chances of becoming church pianist.

Unbuttoning my blouse, I walked into my bedroom to change. When I glanced at the window toward my garden, my hand froze on the middle button.

My plants were drooping.

Fastening my shirt, I raced out the back door toward my garden. Tears pricked my eyes as I approached. Green bean leaves curled. Tomato vines had turned limp and looked the worst of all the plants.

I dropped to my knees and fingered the tomato plant's dying leaves. *Herbicide injury.* Evil Eavesdropper must've doused my garden with weed killer.

My eyes fastened on a metal garden sign and the attached paper rustling in the breeze.

Not again. I bent closer and read the limerick written in red ink.

A mystery for Georgia Rae,
Who jumped right into the fray.
A slippery solution
Demands resolution.
Before her judgment day.

CHAPTER TWENTY

"I'm sorry, Sweet Peach. Is there anything you can do to save the plants?" Yvonne asked. Wearing her aqua bikini top with a striped towel wrapped around her waist, she knelt in the grass and examined the limerick.

"The damage has been done." I covered my face with my hands. "Some of the plants might snap out of it if I irrigate them really well, but the tomatoes are goners."

My mom wouldn't be making salsa with my tomatoes this year.

Yvonne stood and adjusted her towel. "As bad as this is, I'm more worried about the limerick. Sounds like a death threat to me."

"I know." As I reread the poem, my stomach twisted at the third line. *Slippery solution.* Alliteration. Had alliteration-loving Wolfe written the poem?

Or had Jerry Fincher killed the plants? As a farmer, he would have plenty of knowledge about herbicides.

"We'll see what Cal's take is," she said.

I'd called him, and he was on his way. "Even though I'm

creeped out, I sort of feel judged for not figuring out who's messing with me."

Yvonne gaped at me. "That's your takeaway?"

"I'm using bad humor to deal with fear."

"Fair enough. You find anything out from the piano tuner?"

I told her what I'd learned. "Diana must've been really attached to her position to pull a stunt like that on her little sister."

"Sounds like it. The real question is if Arden cared enough to get revenge."

"She might've if she was sick of Diana manipulating her."

Cal arrived and jogged over to where we were standing. He ran his fingers through his hair as he read the message. "You need to back off." He met my eyes.

"I'm not doing anything."

"So you and Mom have been here all day hanging out." He crossed his arms.

"Well—"

"Son, we had a girls' day in Wildcat Springs."

"And this girls' day wouldn't happen to include nosing around for information about Arden Tanner and Diana Graham, would it?"

"People like to tell Georgia things," Yvonne said. "She's got a way about her that makes people want to gab. She can't help that she has cravings for cookies at Pastry Delight and that Bobbi Sue Miller knows all the good gossip. You can't keep your girlfriend locked away in her home."

"I can try when there's a psycho on the loose."

"And Psycho had no trouble breaching her house—or destroying her property." Yvonne pointed at the garden and set her jaw in a way that reminded me of Cal.

Cal looked at his mom. "Will you give us a minute?"

"I'll be lounging by the pond if you need me." She stalked away, with her flip-flops snapping.

"Did Arden Tanner kill her sister?" I asked as soon as Yvonne was out of earshot.

"You know I can't tell you that."

"Could Jerry Fincher be involved?"

"No comment."

"What about Wolfe?"

"Why do you keep asking me questions you know I can't answer?" He scowled.

"Are you going to question Hamlet?"

"No comment."

"I take that as a yes."

"You can take it as *no comment*."

"He didn't do it," I said.

"How do you know?"

"Because I know him. It's the same way I'd be certain of your innocence if you were falsely accused of a crime."

"Because you love me?"

"Yes."

He narrowed his eyes. "So you still love Hamlet?"

"Only as a friend. I was never *in* love with him."

"You sure about that?"

I squeezed the bridge of my nose. "Yes. It's why we broke up," I whispered. "Because I'm in love with you. I don't know what else I have to do to convince you." I turned toward the barn. I might as well get to work, and the grain wasn't going to drive itself to the elevator.

"Georgia."

He caught my hand, and I turned to face him.

"I'm sorry. You don't need to convince me." He wrapped his arms around me. "I love you so much that I can't bear the thought of anything happening to you, and as much as I want to rule out Hamlet, I haven't been able to yet. I'm just doing my job."

"I know." My heart squeezed as I leaned against his muscular chest. Could Hamlet have fooled me? Fooled all of us?

"And I'm not going to rest until we win this game and Evil Eavesdropper is put away for good."

Later that night, after Yvonne and I had returned from the grain elevator, we were getting ready to return to Cal's house for the night when my doorbell rang. We looked at each other and crept toward the door.

"You expecting someone?" Yvonne whispered.

"No." I peeked through the sidelight. "It's my mom."

Yvonne removed her hand from her gun, and I opened the door.

My mom held out a picnic basket as she stepped inside. "I come in peace."

"What've you got?" I asked.

"Comfort food. Meatloaf with potatoes and carrots."

"I'll give you ladies a minute." Yvonne slipped out the front door.

Mom followed me into the dining room and set the basket on the table. "Has Cal figured out who poisoned Austin?"

"Not yet." I told her about the bugs, Diana's murder, and my garden. Her eyes clouded with concern.

"Oh, honey." She drew me into a hug, reached up, and smoothed my hair. "I'm so sorry."

"Cal suspects Hamlet—and a few others."

She stepped back and looked up at me. "Hamlet wouldn't do these awful things to you."

"I know." I picked a hangnail. "Yvonne hasn't left my side,

and I promise I haven't been doing stupid stuff to try to find Evil Eavesdropper, but it feels like I'm not safe anywhere. I'm going to stay in Cal's guest room again tonight, and Gus is still with J.T."

For a second, she looked as if she wanted to argue but thought better of it. "We'll pray that Cal catches the person who's doing this. I overreacted at the hospital, and I'm sorry. Cal's a good man, and if he's your choice, I support you. I just want you to be happy because I love you."

"I love you too."

I just hoped I lived long enough to be happy.

The next morning, Yvonne and I drove into town for the Wildcat Arts Festival. The night before at Cal's house, he, his mother, and I had a long discussion about whether or not I should help Ashley with her booth. We concluded that as long as Yvonne and her nine-millimeter were with me, I'd be as safe at the festival as I'd be at my house, given all of the destruction that'd happened there. Cal figured helping Ashley would keep me occupied so that I *couldn't* poke around.

He was planning to meet Yvonne and me for lunch after we worked in Ashley's booth—if he could get away from work.

The humidity had taken a short hiatus, and the crowd was building as Yvonne and I navigated swarms of people waiting in food booth lines on Main Street. The tempting scent of fried dough lingered on the breeze, and I cast a longing gaze at the Baptist church's blueberry doughnut booth.

After Yvonne's comments yesterday, there was no way I'd be stopping for a snack.

Young couples pushed strollers, and teenagers moved in male and female herds. A few girls wore shorts and tank tops that would never have passed my parents' inspection when I was their age.

We made our way to Sycamore Park where Ashley's tent was located along with other artists' booths. A local cover band was playing "Boys of Summer" in the gazebo.

In spite of my swirling emotions, I was determined to put on a happy face to help my friend, but when Yvonne and I arrived at Ashley's tent, my heart sank when I spotted the blank canvases propped on easels.

Had I agreed to a demonstration? I'd seriously thought we were going to be handing out paintbrushes engraved with her studio's phone number.

Ashley smiled as we entered the tent. "I'm glad you could join us, Ms. Conner." The evening before, I'd given Ashley a tutorial on Yvonne's last name preference.

"Call me Yvonne."

"What do you need us to do?" I was secretly hoping for paintbrush distribution duty.

"Y'all are going to paint a still life of cacti, so people can see how fun my classes are." She pointed at a finished painting with three plants clustered together.

"Where's Brandi?" She wasn't going to miss out on this experience.

"I'm here." She hurried into the booth and greeted Yvonne.

"Perfect." Ashley plunked a sign on the table that read, *Watch us demonstrate a class that you can take at Joy of Imagination Art Studio.* She pointed at the stools arranged in front of each canvas. "Have a seat."

Ashley showed us the first few steps, and I wiped sweat from my forehead and drew my brush through some green paint. I followed her instructions, and soon an oblong blob stared back at me. I sneaked a peek at Brandi's canvas. She was listening intently and had managed to paint something that was already recognizable as a cactus. Yvonne flipped her sandal against her heel and produced a cactus that was far superior to mine—but not as polished as Brandi's.

People had stopped milling past and now gathered in front of Ashley's booth. A few middle school kids walked by and shouted hello to Brandi, and I was certain I heard a few giggles. As happy as I was for Ashley's publicity, I wasn't a fan of people scrutinizing the green splotches I was trying to pass off as cacti.

"Georgia!" My neighbor, Lorelei McPherson, pushed her way to the front of the crowd. I half expected to see her parakeet perched on her shoulder. "Did you ever figure out who vandalized your kitchen?"

"Not yet."

A few people standing nearby gave her curious glances. "You haven't seen anything else strange in our neighborhood, have you?" I asked.

"Not at all, though everybody's been pretty stirred up about Diana Graham's murder. It's hard to think about something like that happening in our sweet little town, but bad things have happened before." Lorelei stepped closer to me. "If I were the cops, I'd be looking into my neighbor, Jerry Fincher."

My hand froze, hovering over green paint. "Why's that?" I tightened my grip on the paintbrush.

"Because Jerry and Diana were dating."

CHAPTER TWENTY-ONE

"R ecently?" I asked Lorelei.

"Diana was at Jerry's house last Friday."

I thought about Diana's date with Wolfe and her alleged preference for younger men. "Are you sure Jerry and Diana weren't just friends?"

"Her car would be at his place overnight, and she always kissed him on the way out in the morning. I'm not talking about a smooch you give a friend—unless he's a friend with benefits." She cupped her hand next to her mouth and leaned closer. "I heard he helped get her that big renovation contract over at the municipal airport, so maybe she was repaying him."

Could they have been working together to get back at me for cash renting the Dillman family's land? Diana could've given him the information about my outdated kitchen. "How long had Jerry and Diana been seeing each other?"

"The first time I noticed Diana at his house was this past winter, but that hasn't stopped her from throwing herself at the rest of the single men in town—young and old." She picked up a paintbrush from Ashley's display table and rolled it between her fingers. "It's possible Jerry got jealous and snapped. Diana was a real piece of work."

I waited a second to see if Lorelei would elaborate, and when she didn't, I pressed forward. "I heard Diana wouldn't let her sister keep her pet parakeet in her rental house, so you adopted it."

"Yep. That's a perfect example of how Diana operated. Although, before she was even cold, Arden called and asked if I'd consider returning Wilbur." The lines in her forehead deepened as if she realized the significance of what she'd said. "You know, the cops should look at Arden. Since Diana didn't have any kids, Arden's likely to inherit all of Diana's property, and she no longer has to abide by the lease that made her give up Wilbur in the first place."

I couldn't disagree with Lorelei's theory. "Are you going to return the bird?"

"Already did. As soon as Wilbur saw Arden, he was over-joyed. His tail and little tongue were shaking, and he chirped more in that few minutes than the whole time he lived with me. I was fine because I'd already figured out owning a bird wasn't my cup of tea." She pointed toward Ashley's canvas. "I'm distracting you. I'm off to get my elephant ear—a late breakfast." She wiggled her fingers and walked away.

I compared my painting to Ashley's model, and I'd fallen hopelessly behind. At least judges weren't evaluating my work. I set my paintbrush aside, grabbed my phone, and slipped between the tent flaps. Even though I was on the back side, dozens of people strolled past, and I held the flap up, so my friends and Yvonne could keep an eye on me.

I dialed Cal's number and waited. When he didn't pick up, I left a voicemail about what I'd learned from Lorelei McPherson. I had a feeling he already knew, but I needed to share every morsel of information I stumbled upon. I made a mental note ask Arden about Diana's relationship with Jerry.

Instead of returning to my easel, I moved to the front of the tent and decided to act as Ashley's carnival barker. I clasped a handful of paintbrushes to distribute as people passed. "Good morning, folks. Give Ashley at Joy of Imagination Art Studio a call if you'd like to participate in one of her fun art classes. They make great date nights."

A while later, I held out a brush to a thin, frazzled looking young woman who was pushing a jogging stroller that held an adorable chubby-cheeked baby I guessed was about nine months old.

The woman took the brush, and as she bent to tuck it into the diaper bag, I noticed her long legs were tan and very toned. In other words, the kind of gams that would make Jerry Fincher proclaim, "Whoo-boy!"

"Ma'am, do you ever jog on 500 North?" I blurted.

"I have been ever since I started training for a half marathon." She eyed me over her sunglasses.

I smiled at the baby. "Did you happen to run by last Tuesday morning between roughly 8:30 and 9:30?"

"I did. Why?"

"I live on the farm between 1000 and 1100 East. The one with the red barn and the grain bins. Someone vandalized my kitchen, and I've been looking for anyone who might've witnessed something unusual that day. I've talked to people who live in the area, and a couple of them recalled seeing a tall woman with a jogging stroller. When I saw yours, I thought I'd ask. Anything you remember might be helpful."

"Right. I'm Chrissy, by the way, and this is Willow." She pointed at the baby. "Let's see. Tuesday. Tuesday. There's the obnoxious man who whistled when I went by." She grimaced. "I thought our society was moving past behavior like that, but apparently he hasn't gotten the memo."

"Anything else?"

Her eyes widened. "Last Tuesday was when I almost got run over. I was headed east, just past your house, when a gray sedan came roaring up behind me. I had to take to the side ditch." Her face twisted with disgust. "Most drivers are careful when they see a runner with a stroller, but not this bozo."

"Did you see the driver?"

"No. We were facing the sun, and I was too busy comforting Willow who was screaming her head off. She'd been sleeping, but the trip into the ditch—and my cussing at the driver—woke her." She glanced down at her daughter. "I did see a Michigan license plate—but couldn't get the number. Sorry."

"No worries. I appreciate your time." What if Wolfe had been renting the car longer than he'd led me to believe when I'd seen him at the airport? Or had Arden not registered her car in Indiana?

As Chrissy walked away, I glanced at my phone. Cal still hadn't called, but Preston had sent a message that he'd be there in a half an hour for lunch—and he was hungry. There was about an hour before the talent show. I texted Cal what I'd learned from Chrissy while Ashley, Brandi, and Yvonne finished their paintings—which looked great. I pointed to my own pathetic cacti. "I'm sorry, Ashley."

"Don't be, hon. You did a lot more for me by talking to the people who were passing." She slipped my canvas behind a table.

Which was a kind way of saying my artistic endeavors would've scared them away.

"Ashley, would you mind if Yvonne and I took a break to eat with Preston?"

"Not at all." She turned to Brandi. "Don't feel like you have to be stuck here all day."

"I don't mind," Brandi said. "I'm not hungry yet since I had a gigantic blueberry doughnut from the Baptist church's booth."

My stomach growled, and I tried not to be jealous.

Yvonne and I slipped through the tent flap, and I told her what Chrissy had said about the car.

"We don't know that the crazy driver came from your house, but it's a lead we should check out," she said.

"I still want to see if we can find Arden at the park—if she's not in custody. She probably has to show up early for the talent show."

"Yvonne's with you, Georgia Peach."

As we walked toward the park, I filled her in on everything Lorelei had shared with me. "I'm wondering if Jerry and Diana were working together to mess with my head—and something went wrong with their relationship."

"That's not a bad theory."

When we arrived at the large gazebo in the center of the park, the temporary bleachers were filling, and folks were setting up lawn chairs. The gazebo held several stand microphones and a grand piano. I led Yvonne to the red and white striped tent behind the gazebo, and as we entered, we dodged three little girls in pink tutus.

It took me a second to recognize Arden without her glasses and plenty of eye makeup, but she sat on a folding chair in the corner observing the chaos in the tent. A woman holding a makeup brush chased one of the tutu girls, and several bored teenagers with their faces in their phones were scattered around.

Arden had adopted a much more glamorous look and wore a sleeveless red sequined dress with a slit that displayed her legs. Her face remained expressionless as Yvonne and I approached.

"I'm sorry about your sister," I said.

"The Wildcat Springs resident sleuth has come to interrogate me about Diana's murder. I'm surprised it's taken you this long."

There was no sense in denying why I was there. "You look nice."

"Your flattery has no impact on me."

"I wouldn't expect it to."

"I'm glad we understand each other." Arden swept her gaze over Yvonne. "You are?"

"Yvonne Conner. Georgia's future mother-in-law."

I really wished she'd quit telling people that.

Arden's face remained stoic as she glanced toward the stage. "I'm playing Aaron Copland's 'The Cat and the Mouse' for the talent show. People need to know I'm capable of performing in front of a crowd. My sister ruined my reputation."

"I'm sorry," I said. "I didn't know when I agreed to play at church last Sunday."

"I'm aware." She glanced at her phone. "The show starts in forty-one minutes. To save you the trouble of asking, I'll give you the condensed version of my experiences at the sheriff's department. I don't have an alibi for the time of Diana's death because she was strangled in the middle of the night. She was a manipulative and controlling woman, but I didn't kill her. If I were going to murder her, I would've poisoned her slowly over time."

Merciful heavens. Maybe she *had* been the one to leave the casserole.

"She was strong and could've fought me while I was strangling her." Arden held out her arms and pointed to her legs. "See? Not a single bruise or scratch."

"You're quite the cool customer, aren't you?" Yvonne said.

"I want justice for Diana because she didn't deserve to die that way. No one does. I'm not upset about being a murder suspect and getting to experience an interrogation firsthand. It's excellent research. I'm a better writer for it." She regarded me. "Georgia Rae will find the truth. She always does."

Was Arden flattering *me* to divert our suspicions? Honestly, it didn't seem like something she'd do. What was her game?

Arden looked back and forth between us. "Is there anything else you want to know? The clock's ticking."

I still had so many questions. "What kind of car do you drive?"

"A red Civic."

Then she probably wasn't the crazy driver, but that didn't mean she wasn't Evil Eavesdropper. "Why'd you move to Wildcat Springs?"

"I broke up with my boyfriend of five years when he refused to marry me. I needed a change, so Diana suggested I come here. It sounded like a nice place to live and write a novel. I didn't realize she'd attempt to control my life."

"How so?" Would Arden confirm what others had told us?

"She forced me to give away my pet parakeet Wilbur." She looked at Yvonne. "I didn't kill my sister over a bird. When my lease was up, I was going to move and get a new parakeet. However, now that Diana has passed, Wilbur is back with me."

Even if Arden didn't kill Diana over Wilbur, I wasn't convinced she didn't have another reason to want her sister dead. "Did you and Diana fight over Wolfe Sommers?"

"No. She had no idea about his interest in me. I didn't say anything about him flirting with me at your house. He didn't ask me on a date until this morning when he called to check on me after hearing about Diana."

"Did you agree to go out with him?" Yvonne asked.

"I did. He's interesting. If nothing comes of our date, I'll develop a character based on him."

How . . . romantic. "Why did Diana pursue Wolfe when she was dating Jerry Fincher?"

"She wasn't. Jerry dumped her last Sunday. She thought she

could annoy Jerry by chasing Wolfe. It didn't work because Jerry didn't care and came to despise her manipulative ways."

"Do you think Jerry could've killed your sister?" I asked.

"Cal really doesn't tell you things, does he?" Arden crossed her legs. "Jerry couldn't have killed Diana because he flew a friend of his to Iowa for a funeral on Wednesday night and didn't return home until Friday morning."

The same morning we'd seen Jerry at the airport.

Yvonne eyed her. "How'd you know that?"

"Because Jerry's friend is my boss Taryn's father."

"Did Diana make you cancel a date with Hamlet Miller?" Yvonne asked.

"No. I changed my mind and blamed Diana."

Yvonne sniffed. "Why's that?"

"There's something too nice about Hamlet. It made me suspicious, and my hesitations were confirmed one day in Latte Conspiracies when I overheard him talking. Diana's dislike of him gave me a perfect excuse to extricate myself from an uncomfortable situation."

I gritted my teeth, trying to ignore Yvonne's triumphant expression.

"We're going to need more information about what you overheard," Yvonne said.

Arden looked at me. "Your boyfriend said the same thing during my interrogation."

"He's very thorough." She was *not* going to get to me.

"Last Friday morning, I went to the coffee shop's restroom and saw Hamlet entering the office. We exchanged pleasantries, and he confirmed our date that night. Then, as I was leaving the ladies' room, I heard him shout from the office, 'I hate her, and she's going to pay for what she's done to me.' His tone was chilling. Later that day, I cancelled our date." She gave me the once over. "I assume he was referring to you."

My heart dropped. Arden had to be toying with us. Hamlet didn't hate me—or want to make me pay for our *mutual* breakup.

"Did you overhear anything else?" Yvonne asked.

"No."

"Did you *see* anyone else?" I gripped the back of a folding chair.

"No. I thought he was on the phone." Arden's cool expression remained unchanged, but I was certain I detected a faint glimmer of malice in her eyes. Could she have designed this grand scheme with the intention of toying with me, killing her sister, and framing Hamlet?

"Do you think Hamlet could've murdered your sister?" Yvonne asked.

"Perhaps. If he wanted to give Georgia Rae a murder mystery to solve as part of an elaborate revenge plot. My sister tried to ruin his reputation, so perhaps he chose her as the victim."

I considered Arden's words—and the limerick's message. *A mystery for Georgia Rae.* How could Arden have known about that—unless she'd written it herself?

"Why on earth would you say that?" I feigned surprise.

Arden blinked. "Lorelei McPherson loves to gossip about the crime in Wildcat Springs. When she returned Wilbur, she told me your kitchen was vandalized."

Cal and I had told Lorelei about the kitchen, but neither one of us had mentioned the limerick. "What does my kitchen vandalism have to do with Hamlet killing your sister to give me a mystery to solve as part of a revenge plot?" I clenched my teeth because I was about ten seconds away from tackling Arden if she didn't tell the whole truth.

"You're abysmal at playing dumb." Arden surveyed me. "Your cheeks are flushed."

Yvonne coughed—loudly.

"Lorelei heard from her nephew who works in the sheriff's

department that when your kitchen was vandalized, someone left a poem about a mystery for you. She also knew about your stepbrother eating a poisoned casserole. Do you deny these events?"

"No." I had to change the conversation's trajectory, but my thoughts were jumbled, and I was finding it hard to focus.

"Did Hamlet ever threaten Diana?" Yvonne asked.

"Not that I know of. However, it seems logical that he could've designed these crimes based on his knowledge of Georgia and her life."

"I agree," Yvonne said.

We had to get away from this Hamlet-as-the-suspect conversation because it was distracting us from finding the real killer, so I landed on the first statement that came to mind. "Taryn said Diana bought a cookie tray for me," I blurted.

Arden tilted her head. "She did. She could be nice. When she went to your house to deliver them, your stepbrother was leaving and told her you weren't home. Since he appeared to be in a hurry, she decided to deliver them later but never had the chance." She studied me. "You're flustered at the thought of Hamlet Miller being guilty, aren't you?"

"She's been arguing with me about it." Yvonne croakled.

"I see." Arden gazed toward the stage—again. "Be careful you don't overlook people close to you, or you might not solve this mystery, Georgia Rae."

A chill passed through my body, and I became certain of one thing. We were done here.

I stood. "Break a leg."

"I don't need luck. I've practiced."

As Yvonne and I left the tent, my phone buzzed with a text from Preston.

I'm here and starving.

"Preston's ready for lunch," I said.

"You want to talk about that conversation?"

"Nope."

"You've got a huge blind spot where Hamlet's concerned."

"It's loyalty to a friend."

"Have it your way," she said.

"Don't mind if I do."

We wound through the park on our way to the United Methodist church parking lot where volunteers were selling chicken and noodle dinners to raise money for missions.

Preston was waiting at the end of the line that stretched outside of the tent and around the church. "They'd better have noodles left," he said as we approached. "Austy wants me to bring him a to-go box."

"I'm sure there's plenty." I scanned the crowd.

He looked back and forth between Yvonne and me. "What's wrong?"

"Nothing. It's all peachy for Georgia Peach."

"I don't believe you," he said.

"She's in a snit and will get over it." Yvonne patted my back. "How's the real estate market around here?"

Preston perked up. "You looking to buy?"

"You never know. I might want to relocate if I have grandbabies someday."

I couldn't even deal with that thought right now. Instead, while Preston tried to land a new client, I took out my phone and sent a text to Hamlet—praying that he had his electronic leash on him, because more often than not he left it in his car.

I need to talk to you right away. Can we meet?

A few seconds later, his response slid onto my screen.

Yes. Holden and I are just leaving the festival. Where?

Preston and Yvonne were still discussing the housing market, so I typed a response.

I'm in the noodle tent line. Meet me in the United Methodist church's sanctuary—A.S.A.P.

I tapped my foot as I waited until my phone buzzed.

Okay. Need to find a parking space.

"I'm going to the restroom," I mumbled as I slipped out of line and hustled toward the church's main entrance.

When I pushed inside the glass double doors, cool air, a hint of old-building mustiness, and silence greeted me. I climbed the carpeted steps and entered the deserted sanctuary. Stained-glass windows adorned the back and side walls, and an ornate wooden pulpit stood next to a matching altar. The room should have felt like a safe haven, but the doubts Arden had planted in my mind sprang up like persistent weeds among my crops. What if Yvonne was right, and I was about to make a huge mistake?

A floorboard creaked. "What's going on, Georgia Rae?"

CHAPTER TWENTY-TWO

I jumped at the sound of Hamlet's voice—even though I'd invited him. He stood in the arched doorway with Holden at his side. Hamlet could often appear inscrutable, and today was no exception. However, Holden wore the same fierce expression my stepbrothers displayed when they were in Georgia Protection Mode.

"I told him to ignore your text," Holden said. "You've already messed up his life enough."

"I don't believe you're guilty." I clutched the back of a pew.

"But Detectives Hawk and Perkins consider me a suspect." Hamlet stepped closer. "They interrogated me last night."

"He had to miss a performance of *The Music Man.*" Holden crossed his arms.

"I'm sorry."

"You should be," Holden said.

"I've told Cal you'd never hurt me—or anyone else. He isn't listening."

Holden glared at me.

Hamlet nudged his brother. "This isn't Georgia's fault. Someone's targeting her and setting me up to take the blame."

"Which means we can't turn against each other," I said.

"I agree. The detectives didn't have enough to hold me, but I was told I can't leave town." He shook his head. "I have to clear my name."

"I know." My phone buzzed with a text from Preston.

Where are you? Yvonne is freaking out.

I'd better answer. "One second, guys," I said as I typed.

Taking care of something. Be back soon. Tell her not to worry.

Shoving my phone into my pocket, I turned my attention to Hamlet. I needed him to tell me what Cal wouldn't—*couldn't*—tell me. "What was Cal focusing on when he questioned you?" I dropped into a pew.

Holden remained in body-guard mode, but Hamlet joined me. "Detective Hawk handled the interrogation and asked me to give an account of my whereabouts the night of Diana's murder," Hamlet said. "I was in my apartment—alone. I was by myself when your house was vandalized, and I don't have an alibi for the time the poisoned casserole was delivered. Apparently, they think I bugged your house."

My stomach tightened. "So you had opportunity and possibly the means. What about motive?"

"From what I could gather, the main theory is that I constructed an elaborate plot designed to torment you and that I chose to murder Diana because she tried to ruin my business reputation—and my chance of dating her sister Arden. I told them she cancelled our date, but I blew it off and moved on because she's not the kind of woman I'm looking for."

No kidding. "She told me she overheard you at Latte Conspiracies saying, 'I hate her, and she's going to pay for what she's done to me.' And she told Cal and Vanessa that, which must be why they questioned you."

Hamlet closed his eyes and groaned. "I was rehearsing for my movie role. I'm playing a jilted lover."

"He's telling the truth," Holden said. "I've seen the script—and helped him run the lines."

My mind raced. "If we can't prove Hamlet didn't do these things, then we need to prove who did."

"How?" Holden asked.

The three of us stared at each other in silence.

"It's too bad Gus can't talk." Hamlet chuckled ruefully. "He knows exactly who's been in and out of your house—and it's not me."

Gus.

"Holden, when you delivered the beef heart last Sunday morning, my dog was barking like crazy, right?"

"Uh-huh. It was weird because I wasn't even close to your back porch, and he was going nuts. I could hear him as soon as I got out of my car."

"Did you notice anything else strange that morning?"

"Uhh . . . now that you mention it, a gray car came out of your driveway. I thought someone had gotten lost and was turning around."

"A sedan?"

"Yeah."

"Do you think the person driving that car had been in your house?" Hamlet asked.

"Yes—I think the driver could be the Evil Eavesdropper, who'd been there bugging my house. Cal told me all of the bugs still had battery life, so they hadn't been there all that long. Last Sunday morning, on the way to church, a gray car nearly sideswiped me. Then, a woman who regularly runs on my road reported a gray car nearly ran her over the same day my house was vandalized. When I ran into Wolfe Sommers picking up Liza Bell at the airport on Thursday, he was driving a gray sedan because his car was being repaired."

"He was telling the truth," Hamlet said. "I saw the damage to his Miata myself when he needed a ride from the scene on Wednesday evening, and I was the one who took him to the airport so he could get the rental car—and Liza—on Thursday."

A rental car.

If Wolfe had been driving his Miata until Wednesday night, then someone else must've borrowed the gray sedan from the rental car company in the terminal.

My heart plummeted as I reconsidered my other assumptions —and something else Arden had told me. I shot to my feet and darted into the aisle. "I need to make a quick call. Excuse me!"

Removing my phone from my pocket, I ran out of the sanctuary. Tapping Austin's number, I hurried outside, squinted in the sunlight, and shaded my eyes. I had to find Yvonne and Preston but didn't see them in the tent.

Austin answered. "Hey, sissy!"

"Did you talk to Diana Graham at my house on Wednesday afternoon and tell her I wasn't home when she came to deliver cookies?" I blurted.

"No."

"You're positive."

"Yes! I remember everything that happened that day, and I definitely didn't see Diana Graham—or any cookies."

My stomach tightened. That meant Diana Graham had accidentally run into Evil Eavesdropper when he was leaving my house after delivering the poisoned casserole, which meant Evil

Eavesdropper might not have planned to kill Diana—unless she figured out that he wasn't my brother.

"What's going on?" he asked.

"I'll tell you later, but a gray sedan rented at the Richardville Airport is important." I disconnected and scanned the crowd in the tent and parking lot. No Preston. No Yvonne. In the distance, I heard Arden playing "The Cat and the Mouse" for the talent show. Her parting words echoed in my mind.

"Be careful you don't overlook people close to you, or you might not solve this mystery, Georgia Rae."

Arden was right—and it all had to do with the airport.

Diana had been finishing her renovation of the airport offices on Sunday, the first day I'd seen the gray sedan and the same day Holden had reported seeing it leave my driveway. Diana must've seen—and heard—Evil Eavesdropper at the rental car counter and was dead because after attempting to deliver the cookies, she'd figured out Evil Eavesdropper wasn't my stepbrother—as he'd claimed.

Poor Diana had been a loose end in a game designed to torment me, frame Hamlet for my impending murder, and ultimately hurt Cal.

I stepped under the shade of a tree and tapped Cal's number. "Pick up, Cal."

Arden finished playing, and the audience applauded.

I curled my fingers into a ball. There was only one person who'd be motivated to hurt me to torment Cal, who might've used the rental car agency at the airport—and who could pass as one of my stepbrothers.

Would Cal believe me? Or would he think my conclusion was a last-ditch effort to save Hamlet? The phone continued ringing. "Pick up, Cal!" I hissed.

"Hello, Georgia Rae."

My heart dropped at the sound of Mason's voice on the line.

CHAPTER TWENTY-THREE

"Where's Cal?" I demanded.

"Busy. But you'll see him soon."

Squeezing my eyes shut, I wished with everything in me that I'd been wrong about Mason. *Jesus, help Cal.* "What've you done?"

"You should see the look on your face," Mason said. "Terrified and confused, yet you look cute in that little red top."

A chill trickled down my spine. I whipped around, scanning the church's parking lot in search of Mason. But I didn't see him.

"Listen closely, and do everything I say."

Preston's warning reverberated in my mind. *"Don't you even think about, for one second, giving yourself up to this psycho."* I set my jaw. "Or what?"

"Or I'm going to set off the IED under the table in your best friend's booth."

I froze.

"Walk down the alley between the historical society and the funeral home."

I hurried across the parking lot and slipped into the alley

behind a dumpster. "How do I know you aren't bluffing?" Even as I said the words, I realized how stupid they were. Mason was completely capable of building an IED—he'd disarmed them in Afghanistan.

"Do you really want me to kill your two best friends and other innocent people because you refuse to believe me?"

"No." My voice trembled.

"I'm glad we agree. If I see you so much as blink at anyone, the booth goes boom. Now cross Pearl Street and keep walking toward the high school parking lot."

I paused at the end of the alley. A few people were exiting the parking lot and walking down Pearl Street toward the booths on Main. "There are a lot of people here, and I'm bound to run into someone I know," I whispered. "What then?"

"Wave and don't stop walking. You're on the phone, so they won't bother you. Your friends' lives depend on you doing exactly as I say."

Where could Mason be that he could see me clearly yet be able to talk freely without someone hearing? He had to be behind me. Praying I'd run into Yvonne and Preston, I followed the sidewalk on Pearl Street, but I didn't know the few people I passed.

"Why are you doing this?" I hissed as I darted across the street.

Silence.

"I'm at the parking lot. Now what?"

"See the row of cars next to the Sycamore trailhead?"

"Yes."

"Walk toward the gray sedan with the Michigan plate and stop. Don't turn around."

I obeyed, but my heart dropped when I got closer to the car and spotted a dog crate wedged into the back seat. "Gus."

"You didn't think your dog would be completely safe with your cousin when he works all the time, did you?"

Gus whined as I opened the door. "Why're you doing this, Mason?" I peered through the crate. My dog woofed but appeared unharmed.

"Get in and start the engine."

I obeyed.

Mason opened the passenger door and held a gun so I could see. "Give me your phone." When I handed it over, he used his free hand to disconnect, set it on his lap, and wipe off my phone and Cal's with a bleach wipe. Then he tossed them into the bushes. "Drive." He got in and slammed the door.

I put the car in reverse. "Where?"

"Cal's house."

"Is he there?"

"Yes. And if you even think about trying to get someone's attention, I'll shoot your dog and blow up your friends." He wiggled a flip phone that I assumed could act as a detonator.

Death-gripping the steering wheel, I drove through the parking lot and onto the road. "Why're you doing this?"

"Did Cal ever give you the full story of why he left Cleveland?"

"He said he'd always wanted to have a small hobby farm."

"That's true—and it's the excuse he gave me when he moved. But it's not the full story."

I stopped at an intersection and waited on the traffic to pass. Could I believe anything Mason said? "Then what don't I know?"

"My wife was in love with him."

I was nearly certain my heart had stopped beating for good, but a split second later it thumped on. "He never told me that." Had Cal had an affair with Natalie? No. He wouldn't do that, but I forced myself to ask the obvious question. "Was he in love with *her*?"

"No. And in case you're wondering, he never took advantage

of her feelings—even though he could have, because she told him how she felt."

"When did you find out?" I drove through the intersection.

"About a week after Natalie died, I read her journals hoping to get a clue about what happened to her. Instead, I learned how heartbroken and humiliated she was when Cal moved. Imagine being a grieving husband, and the wife you adored had been wallowing for months behind your back because she was in love with your best friend, and he'd moved away—and had a new girlfriend."

"Did you kill her?" I asked.

"Of course not!" He scowled. "I didn't know about any of this until after she died, remember? Think how stupid I felt. Years of being relieved that her date with Cal didn't go well, and I got my chance. But she wanted *him* all along."

I found it hard to believe Mason didn't have any idea, but maybe she'd worked hard to hide her feelings. "I still don't understand why you'd want to hurt Cal and me." I glanced at him out of the corner of my eye.

"You're smart. I'll give you one guess as to how Natalie dealt with her grief over Cal moving away and finding you."

"She rode her bike," I whispered.

"That's right. I'd warned her time and time again that trail was too dangerous for her to ride by herself, but it was an unseasonably warm day, and she went out anyway."

"Mason, I'm so, so sorry she died."

"I am too."

"But Cal didn't kill your wife, so you don't need to hurt us. Please just stop for your son's sake. He needs you."

"I don't intend to get caught. That's what Hamlet's for."

I couldn't let him ruin Hamlet's life too. "Did you kill Diana Graham because she saw you at my house—and the airport?" I fixed my eyes on the road.

"Even though I have blond hair and blue eyes like your step-brothers, it was only a matter of time until that busybody figured out that I wasn't Austin. She'd seen me at the rental car counter on Sunday. Little flirt gave me the once over. I wasn't going to let her derail my plans for you and Cal, so I hid in her backyard, and when she took her dog out, I solved my problem. I knew I could use her death in the game I'm playing with you, because what fun is a mystery without a murder?"

Poor Diana. She really had been in the wrong place at the wrong time.

I glanced at Mason out of the corner of my eye. His posture was rigid, his jaw clenched.

"Why write limericks?" I asked.

"Nat used to leave them for me. She loved words—and being silly."

"She wrote the poems to show how much cared. She wouldn't want you to do this."

"You didn't know her!" he growled.

"No." I slowed and turned onto Cal's and my road. "But you won't get away with this. You've left a trail flying in and out of the airport—and renting a car."

He dug into his back pocket, produced his wallet, and flipped it open. I glanced at the name on the driver's license. *Rodney Stockton.* "I took care of that problem. I have the money—and connections."

I swallowed. "What about God?"

"What about him, Georgia Rae? God took my wife, and instead of letting me grieve like a normal husband and live with my happy memories, he had to show me my entire marriage was a sham."

"How long have you been planning this?"

"When Cal went into a tailspin after that letter claimed Natalie's death was about revenge, I figured I could hurt him even worse if he got back together with you, and I found a way to make your lives miserable. I encouraged him not to deny the good things God might want to give him. Once he told me you were back together, I went to work. I've been staying in Richardville for the past week and keeping tabs on you. Once I put the tracker on your truck, it was easy to know when to go into your house."

"Did you bug my house on Sunday morning?"

"Yes. I wanted to gather as much information about you as possible in order to know who to frame for your death. It didn't take me long to figure out Hamlet was the best choice. After I heard how much you freaked out about the stupid beef heart, I knew it'd be fun to play more pranks on you. You love chasing mysteries."

"So you broke into my best friend's house."

"When Brandi left early in the morning for work, and I circled around and went in through her back door with the key I'd copied from your house. I grabbed a sticky note and even used one of her recipes."

"You're sick."

"Everything you're getting is what Cal deserves."

"But Cal didn't have an affair with your wife." I entered Cal's driveway and parked in front of his garage.

"He might as well have because the end result was the same. He took her from me." He held up the detonator. "Now take the dog out of the crate and get into the house."

I freed Gus and didn't wait around to be told again. Clutching the dog's leash while he tugged me along, I ran through the front door. "Cal!"

Miss Peacock woofed and scuttled toward Gus and me. She pawed my legs and whined while Gus sniffed her.

"He's upstairs." Mason pressed the gun into my back.

With the dogs trotting along, I rushed upstairs. What would I find when I got there? *Please God, don't let Cal be dead.*

Holding my breath, I entered the bedroom. With eyes closed, Cal lay sprawled on his bed, his wrists handcuffed to the metal headboard and his legs shackled to the footboard. I raced to his side and checked his pulse.

Steady.

"Cal, wake *up*." I gently patted his cheek while Miss Peacock and Gus rested their paws on the edge of the bed and barked. "Come on."

His eyes opened, then widened. "No. Georgia," he whispered. "Mason—"

"I know." I looked over my shoulder, but Mason wasn't there. Hadn't he been following me?

"You don't under—"

Downstairs, a door slammed. Gus woofed, and Miss Peacock yelped as I darted to the window and shoved the curtain aside. Mason was jogging toward his car.

"Georgia. Listen to me." Cal moaned.

I threw open the window. "Mason!" Our guard dogs stood on their hind legs, resting their paws on the sill.

Mason looked up and waved the flip phone. "You have a big choice to make, Georgia Rae. Better hurry."

Gus barked.

My breath caught as I understood Mason's meaning. The real bomb was *here*—not at the festival. I whirled around and faced Cal. "Where's the bomb?" My voice trembled.

"Behind you."

I turned. "Oh, Lord help us."

The bomb—with a cellphone detonator—poked out from beneath the chest of drawers.

CHAPTER TWENTY-FOUR

For a few seconds, I remained frozen in place as my mind spun. Mason could make the call and set off the bomb at any second.

"Georgia, take the dogs and get out," Cal said.

"I'm not leaving you."

"There might not be enough time to free me." He tugged his restraints. "We don't both have to die."

"Why not?" I choked back a sob. "We'll be in heaven—together." I inspected the headboard, but for all of Cal's tugging, it remained intact.

"If we both die, Mason could get away with this. He told me he planted evidence in Hamlet's apartment to frame him."

"I could detach the bomb and throw it out the window."

"No. He'd anticipate that, and it'll detonate."

"Even if I take off the cellphone?"

"Sweetheart, Mason knows his stuff, and I'm certain he planned for any tampering. Now take the dogs and go find someone to call for help. I love you too much to risk letting you die with me."

My throat thickened. "There has to be another way."

Please, God. Help me think.

Then I remembered sitting in Brandi's parents' basement trying to get a cell signal. *"Between the brick exterior and metal roof this house is a fortress."*

"I can block the cellphone's signal to buy time," I said.

Hope dawned in his expression. "With what?"

I glanced around, then darted into the bathroom. The metal trashcan. Snatching it, I returned to the bedroom. "This." I detached the domed lid.

"That might not be enough."

"We have to try." I removed the drawers from the chest before easing the furniture piece onto its side. I placed the half-moon shaped can's flat side against the floor and carefully maneuvered the open end over the bomb. "What do you think?"

He pointed to the attic door. "Get some fiberglass insulation out of the attic. There's an extra batt."

I yanked open the attic door and snatched a roll of pink, fiberglass insulation. Unrolling it, I placed a triple layer over the trashcan and stuffed the rest into the empty drawer space. "Please let this work, God."

"Amen. Now take the dogs and get out."

"I'm coming back with bolt cutters."

"I'd rather you flag down a car and have the driver call 9-1-1."

Tears welled in my eyes. "I love you." I leaned over and kissed him.

"I love you too." Resolve had settled in his expression. "Take that pen and pad off the nightstand."

"Why?" I picked them up.

"Because I know you're going to come back in after me even though I told you not to, and in case something goes wrong, I want you to stick a note in one of the dog's collars saying Mason did this—and killed Diana."

"Gotcha." I quickly wrote, *Mason Thrailkill (alias Rodney Stockton) set the bomb and strangled Diana Graham.*

"Now go."

I couldn't move. What if the trashcan and insulation didn't work? Would I be able to live with myself? A mental picture of my bleak future stretched before me, engulfing me with horror.

No. Be strong and take heart, all you who hope in the Lord.

I remained frozen.

"Georgia Rae Winston, take those dogs and get out right now!"

His sharp words dragged me from my stupor. Choking back a sob, I scooped up Miss Peacock and tucked the note in her collar. "I'll be back." I grabbed Gus's leash, and with the Schnauzer on my hip, I pounded downstairs and out the door. While I raced across the yard, I listened for the sound of a car on the road but heard nothing.

Ensuring the note was intact, I shut Miss Peacock and Gus in the barn, and a yapping and howling contest ensued. If Cal and I didn't survive, someone would find them.

With a new surge of hope, I ignored my hands that were starting to itch from the insulation and sprinted into Cal's garage. I made a beeline for his work bench where I found a pair of bolt cutters. Since I still didn't hear a vehicle, I thundered inside and up the stairs.

"Did you call 9-1-1?" Cal asked.

I cut his leg shackles. "No one was driving by, but our messenger Miss Peacock and her sidekick Gus are safe in the barn."

"You didn't have to come back."

"Yes. I did."

I freed his hands, and he stood, swaying.

"Are you dizzy?"

"I'll be fine. Let's go."

Draping his arm over my shoulder, I guided him out of the room and down the stairs. He stumbled, but I gripped the railing and steadied him.

"Leg's asleep," he said.

Feeling as if we were moving in slow motion, I led us toward the front door. Onto the porch. Down the steps. Across the yard. And behind the barn where we collapsed into the grass in front of the door. The dogs must've worn themselves out, because I only heard intermittent whines.

Cal wrapped his strong arms around me.

I buried my face in his shoulder, though I was too numb to cry. "Thank you, God," I whispered.

"I wouldn't be too thankful yet." Mason aimed his gun at us.

CHAPTER TWENTY-FIVE

"The bomb should've detonated," Mason said. "What happened?"

Gripping hands, Cal and I stood.

"I made my choice," I said.

"I gave you too much time." Mason's face reddened.

Cal squeezed my hand, and my heart sank. I figured he was planning to tackle Mason to give me an opportunity to get away, but I wasn't going to let him take a bullet for me—not if I could help it.

"Walk back toward the house," Mason said.

Cal flinched. I took a deep breath and prayed Cal would sense what I was about to do. I let loose a vocal cord damaging scream.

Mason froze for a split second. Cal leaped forward and tackled him to the ground while I reached backward and thew open the barn door. The dogs hurtled out as Mason nearly lost his grip on the gun before he bucked upward, slamming his forehead against Cal's nose. Cal recoiled, but Gus and Miss Peacock dove onto Mason. Gus chomped Mason's calf, and he shrieked when Miss Peacock sank her teeth into his forearm.

Cal wrenched the gun from Mason's grasp and scrambled to his feet.

"Get these dogs away from me!" Mason swore.

Before Cal or I could respond, two cars vroomed into the driveway and skidded to a stop. Car doors slammed, and Yvonne, Preston, and Vanessa sprinted toward us. In the distance, sirens wailed.

"Good boy. Good girl." Yvonne yelled as she and Preston restrained the growling dogs while Vanessa handcuffed Mason and led him away.

"You'd better buy these pups of yours some nice treats," Yvonne said.

Cal embraced me and kissed the top of my head while the dogs swarmed us. "We will, Mom. We sure will."

That night, Cal, Yvonne, Preston, Austin, and I gathered in my living room. Miss Peacock sat in Cal's lap, and Gus refused to move from my feet. Outside, a thunderstorm rumbled but brought much needed rain to my crops.

"How'd you know to bring Vanessa with you to Cal's house?" I asked Preston and Yvonne.

She eyed me. "When you disappeared, Preston and I were searching for you. We saw Hamlet, who told us you'd been talking, and you'd asked questions about a gray rental car from the airport and then darted out of the sanctuary to make a call. I figured you'd stumbled onto something."

"Meanwhile, I called Austin to see if he'd heard from you, and he told me how you'd asked about Diana trying to bring cookies and claiming that she'd seen one of us," Preston said.

"Then I got to thinking about who might've used the airport rental car service and could try to pass as Georgia's stepbrother, and Mason came to mind." Yvonne said. "I didn't want to tell Cal I suspected his buddy, but when I couldn't get him on the phone, my gut screamed that something was wrong. I called Vanessa, and she said he'd gone home to let Miss Peacock out. When I told her my theory, she said she'd meet us here." Yvonne scratched Gus's head. "And you know the rest of the story."

We sat in silence for a few seconds listening to the patter of rain against the roof.

"I want you all to know that I never had an affair with Natalie." Cal looked directly into my eyes. "I just . . . never said anything about her feelings for me because I was embarrassed . . . and I didn't think there was any point mentioning it since she'd died."

I squeezed his hand.

"When she shared her feelings with me, I told her I wasn't interested, that Mason loved her, and that she needed to focus on her marriage. That's when I became even more certain that I was ready to move away, so I did. I still felt guilty, though." He swallowed. "I can't believe Mason would do something this awful."

"Heartbreak can do funny things to people," Yvonne said.

It certainly could.

A week after Mason's arrest, Yvonne had returned home, and our lives had settled down, though I knew it would take a while for Cal to heal from Mason's betrayal. He and I were committed to praying for him every day.

I was ready for a drama-free existence with Gus at my side. I'd still have the excitement of my kitchen renovation, but after everything I'd been through, living in a construction zone was minor, and Hamlet was scheduled to begin work on Monday.

Besides, it wasn't like I cooked all that much. My cereal and I were doing just fine.

Tonight, Cal and I would be joining our small group friends for a party Evan was throwing in honor of his girlfriend Kelsey coming home from Ethiopia. Cal picked me up a little before seven.

"You look hot." He grinned, his heart-stopping dimple making an appearance.

My cheeks warmed as I smoothed my sundress's skirt. "You look very handsome yourself."

He helped me into his Jeep, and we drove into Wildcat Springs to Ashley's art studio. As we climbed the stairs to the second floor, the building was unnaturally quiet.

"Are we the first ones here?" I asked. "I seriously thought we were going to be late."

Cal didn't answer but pushed open the door to the large room that overlooked downtown Wildcat Springs. A pink rose petal path led toward a wooden arch strung with white lights and adorned with flowers.

I froze. "I thought we were having a party for Kelsey."

"Not quite." He took my hand and led me toward the canopy. "I have something I need to ask you." We stopped underneath, and he took my other hand.

He was about to propose. This was it. Ring the bells and sound the alarms. Georgia Rae Winston wasn't going to die an old maid.

Life Lesson #18: Miracles really do happen.

"Georgia, you're absolutely astounding. You saved my life and have made it better than I ever dreamed it could be." He bent down on one knee.

I covered my hand with my mouth, because if I hadn't, I'd

have been one of those women who blurted out *yes* before her man even asked.

"Will you marry me?" His dimple appeared.

"Yes!"

He slipped a gorgeous rock on my finger and drew me into a heart-stopping kiss. After he broke away, he shouted, "She said *yes*. Come on out so we can party!"

There was cheering, and Brandi, Ashley, J.T., Kelsey, Evan, David, and Heather filed out of Ashley's office.

Kelsey, Cal's cute and petite cousin, bounced over and hugged me. "I'm so glad you're marrying my cousin." She squealed, took my hand, and surveyed my engagement ring. "Cal did good."

I laughed. "I know. Did you plan this?"

Her blue eyes sparkled. "I did. Cal emailed a few weeks ago and said he needed my help with the perfect proposal. The girls and I decorated and planned the food, and we thought if Evan invited you to a party for me, you'd have no idea anything was up."

"You got me."

Across the room, Brandi, Ashley, and Heather were setting out sandwich, fruit, and vegetable platters on an empty table. J.T. and Evan were selecting music, and David was running around snapping pictures.

Cal came up behind me and squeezed my shoulders.

"This is perfect," I said.

"I wanted to include your friends because I know how important they are to you. Hamlet would've been here too, but he's performing tonight and made me promise to send pictures."

That was sweet of him. I hoped he'd find the right woman someday, because he deserved to be happy. Tears welled in my eyes. "Thank you—for all of this."

"You're welcome." He leaned over and whispered in my ear. "Just so you know, I'm hoping for a short engagement."

I wrapped my arms around him and gazed into his handsome face. "How about December?"

EPILOGUE

A December wedding suited me for several reasons. First, harvest was over and done with, planting was a ways off, and I didn't need either of those seasons hanging over my head while trying to enjoy the day I'd dreamed about forever.

Second, I purchased a lace-sleeved wedding gown that hid my pasty arms. This girl had never been a fan of strapless dresses, because no one needed to see me spending my wedding day adjusting myself for fear of a wardrobe-malfunction.

Third, Cal's church had some wonderful ladies who knew how to pull out all the stops when it came to decorating the sanctuary for Christmas, and they'd saved me a ton of time and money.

Back in October, they'd dragged me into the storage room after church one Sunday, hefted five large plastic totes off a shelf, and showed me all of the possible color schemes they could use for adorning the trees—yes, *trees*. When I told them burgundy would fit nicely with my color scheme, they'd been thrilled. Apparently, the burgundy bulbs hadn't made an appearance for several years and were awaiting their turn in the rotation, so all was right with the committee.

Fourth, it was a busy time of year, and I figured anyone who took the trouble to attend my wedding cared about being there. After waiting and praying for a husband for years, the last thing I wanted was for people to begrudgingly share in my joyous day because they'd rather be wrapping presents, baking cookies, or waiting in line for their child to take a turn being terrified of Santa.

Still, when my big day came, none of that mattered. All I cared about was that at a little past five o'clock, I'd be Mrs. Cal Perkins.

My guests had gathered in Liberty Christian Church, and Brandi, Ashley, and I waited in the basement for Heather—the wedding-day coordinator—to tell us it was time for the ceremony. Kelsey was back overseas and planning to watch via a live stream that Evan had set up for us.

"Are you nervous?" Ashley held out my bouquet of red roses, holly leaves and berries, evergreens, and pinecones.

"No. I feel peaceful."

Brandi smoothed her burgundy gown. "I've been praying."

"That explains it," I said.

Tears flooded Brandi's eyes. "I'm so happy for you and Cal."

My heart squeezed. When would Brandi find someone to spend her life with? It had to be hard watching Ashley and me get engaged to our dream men. And Brandi was even older than both of us. It would be easy, in my joy, to tack on a flippant statement about how she'd find someone someday.

But there were no guarantees, and I was certain no one knew that better than Brandi. It was probably better to ask God to help her accept his plan—whatever that might be.

The door opened, and Heather popped her head in. "It's go time."

Ashley trotted out. Before Brandi followed, she gave me a reassuring smile, almost as if she realized I'd been worrying about her.

I walked up the stairs and took Grandpa Winston's arm while Heather adjusted my train. My friends walked the aisle to "Jesu, Joy of Man's Desiring." When the doors opened, Grandpa and I stepped through to the strains of "Trumpet Voluntary."

Even though Cal and I had taken a private first look before our pictures, my heart still jumped at the sight of him standing at the altar.

In a blur, Pastor Jim married us, and after greeting our guests, Cal and I piled into a limo to go to the reception. It took me a little bit to realize we weren't headed for the fancy reception hall in Richardville that Dan had insisted that we rent. Was our driver abducting us?

"Um. Cal?"

"Yes?" His eyes twinkled.

"Where is the driver taking us?"

"You'll see." He kissed me. "We're not being kidnapped."

"Good to know." I grinned. I wasn't going to even deny thinking it. The driver turned, and when I peeked out the window, I knew where we were going.

"I thought you might like to make a stop, and I even asked the florist to make something special." He opened a box and removed a smaller version of my bridal bouquet.

The driver entered the cemetery and parked near the place where we'd laid Daddy to rest. Cal took my hand and held a camping lantern in the other. Though it was dark, the soft light illuminated our path to Daddy's headstone.

"I wish he could've been with us today," Cal said.

I bent and placed the bouquet on my daddy's grave. When I straightened, Cal put his arm around me.

"Years ago, he told me he was praying that God would bring

the right man into my life for me to marry." I leaned into my husband. "God's answer is even better than I could've imagined."

He kissed the top of my head.

Hand-in-hand, we returned to our limousine, and as we drove to the reception, I said a silent prayer of thanks.

In spite of the heartbreak I'd endured, God had been truly faithful to me.

I hope you've enjoyed Georgia's adventures. Even though her story has come to a close, I'm working on a new mystery series. I hope you'll stay in touch by subscribing to my e-mail newsletter at my website, so you can get the latest on all my new releases.

As a thank you for subscribing, you'll gain access to *Deadly Homestead: A Georgia Rae Winston Mini-Mystery and Other Short Stories.*

If you enjoyed *Deadly Heartbreak*, I'd be very grateful if you'd leave a short review to help me spread the word about my novels.

ABOUT THE AUTHOR

Jenni Mansell Photography

Marissa Shrock is a survivor of many awkward blind dates and many years of teaching middle school. Both provide excellent inspiration for her fictional yarns.

Since childhood, she's loved to read a variety of genres, so her own work includes dystopian thrillers and cozy mysteries. She's the author of the Emancipation Warriors Series and the Georgia Rae Winston Mystery Series. Her debut novel, *The First Principle*, was a Carol Award Finalist.

Marissa enjoys playing golf, building elaborate LEGO creations, and traveling to new places. Her home is in Indiana, where she's surrounded by corn and soybean fields. Visit her at www.marissashrock.com.

CREDITS

Editing by A Little Red Ink

Cover Art by Seedlings Design Studio

Marketing Copy by JR2 Marketing & Advertising

Cimelia Press Logo by Race Point

Beta Readers: Mary Shrock, Brad Shrock, and Katie Briggs

www.ingramcontent.com/pod-product-compliance
Lightning Source LLC
Chambersburg PA
CBHW072052170626
46813CB00004B/1319

9780996987974